Readers love the Royal Navy
series by LEE ROWAN

I0525118

Ransom

"I literally couldn't put it down. It gripped me from start to end. I found it intense, the historical detail well researched and richly scripted."

—Prism Book Alliance

"I thoroughly enjoyed this story. Lee Rowan did a fabulous job of putting me right there with the characters, and I feel like I experienced everything right along with them."

—The Novel Approach

Winds of Change & Eye of the Storm

"The writing is smooth, well-edited, and plenty of sailor lingo and ship terminology to add to the adventure."

—MM Good Book Reviews

Home is the Sailor

"I would definitely recommend *Home is the Sailor* to someone new to Male/Male romance… because the terrific story, great characters, and gorgeous writing will captivate any discerning reader."

—Fresh Fiction

Sail Away

"All of these stories are well-written and quite informative… I do recommend it to fans, who, like me, can't get enough of Davy and Will."

—Rainbow Book Reviews

By LEE ROWAN

Published by DREAMSPINNER PRESS
http://www.dreamspinnerpress.com

Walking Wounded

LEE ROWAN

Published by
DREAMSPINNER PRESS

5032 Capital Circle SW, Suite 2, PMB# 279, Tallahassee, FL 32305-7886 USA
http://www.dreamspinnerpress.com/

This is a work of fiction. Names, characters, places, and incidents either are the product of author imagination or are used fictitiously, and any resemblance to actual persons, living or dead, business establishments, events, or locales is entirely coincidental.

Walking Wounded
© 2015 Lee Rowan.

Cover Art
© 2015 Reese Dante.
http://www.reesedante.com
Cover content is for illustrative purposes only and any person depicted on the cover is a model.

All rights reserved. This book is licensed to the original purchaser only. Duplication or distribution via any means is illegal and a violation of international copyright law, subject to criminal prosecution and upon conviction, fines, and/or imprisonment. Any eBook format cannot be legally loaned or given to others. No part of this book may be reproduced or transmitted in any form or by any means, electronic or mechanical, including photocopying, recording, or by any information storage and retrieval system, without the written permission of the Publisher, except where permitted by law. To request permission and all other inquiries, contact Dreamspinner Press, 5032 Capital Circle SW, Suite 2, PMB# 279, Tallahassee, FL 32305-7886, USA, or http://www.dreamspinnerpress.com/.

ISBN: 978-1-63216-699-9
Digital ISBN: 978-1-63216-700-2
Library of Congress Control Number: 2015904662
Third Edition May 2015
First Edition published by Linden Bay Romance, 2007.
Second Edition published by Cheyenne Publishing/Bristlecone Pine Press, 2009.

Printed in the United States of America

This paper meets the requirements of
ANSI/NISO Z39.48-1992 (Permanence of Paper).

To P, as always... with many thanks to Ann, Ruth, and Sherry for the British perspective on the English language and environs.

Author's Note

"England and America are two countries separated by the same language…"
—George Bernard Shaw

To anyone perplexed by Britspeak, I recommend this site: http://resources.woodlands-junior.kent.sch.uk/customs/questions/glossary/#B

Chapter One

"JOHNNY?"

For a moment John's voice froze, and so did his hand on the telephone receiver. Then he asked cautiously, "Kevin?" It couldn't be, couldn't be. He hadn't heard that voice in years. Where had the time gone? But there was no one else who ever called him that. He had always been "John" to everyone else, or "Lieutenant," or now just "Mr. Hanson."

"Yeah, it's me."

The silence stretched out so long that he was almost ready to add audio hallucinations to the list of his afflictions. But then Kevin said, "Would… would you mind very much if I stopped by?"

John's throat closed up at that, and his eyes filled with tears. Damn the old emotional hair trigger! He hadn't had this strong a reaction to anything for longer than he could remember. "No," he finally managed. "No, of course not. When?"

He heard a deep sigh at the other end of the line and realized this must be just as hard for Kevin as it was for him. Worse, maybe—Kev would've had to get up the nerve to make the call and risk being turned away.

"I can be there tonight," Kevin suggested. "Say by eight? And if you could recommend a hotel—"

"Nonsense. You'll stay here." John bit his lip, wondering if he'd said too much, if the offer would be misinterpreted. Or not. "I mean—there's room enough, I have one of those futons. It's not too lumpy." He pushed aside the image of Kevin sprawled on dark blue sheets, relaxed and sleepy. No. Forget it. That was part of the past now. What they'd had between them was over. But maybe there could still be friendship.

"Oh." Was that disappointment, or relief? "That would be fine, thanks."

"Right. Um… I'm in Portsmouth, you know. You found my number—do you need the address or directions?"

"No, I can find you. Just thought I should ring first. But if you'd rather not be bothered—"

"*No!*" His vehemence surprised and embarrassed him. "No, of course, not, I—" Damn these tears too! "It's… it's good to hear your voice."

"Yours too. I'll be there soon, Johnny." Such a world of promise in the soft tones—a ray of light, a lifeline.

John cradled the receiver gently, then dropped onto the sofa and closed his eyes. His mind flew back to that afternoon in officers' training school, the first session of a class on biological weapons. It was just another class, one he really did not want to take and hoped he'd never have occasion to use. But he'd skimmed through the textbook and had his notebook at the ready. He was good at the academic side of military training; this was just another class.

Until Kendrick, K. walked in and gave his name to the instructor.

There was something about the man, the way he carried himself, that caught John's attention immediately. Then the new student ran his crystal-blue eyes down the row of desks and spotted the empty one just behind Hanson, J. He looked up, their eyes met— and John's breath caught in his throat as his heart started beating wildly. *It's him. He's the one. My God, of all places—it's him!*

He forced himself to look polite rather than poleaxed, and gave a casual nod and smile. The new student blinked once, took his seat, and the instructor started his lecture before anything more could be said, while John thanked whatever deity was in charge that there were no students whose names fell between theirs.

How was this possible? All his life—since puberty, anyway— he had been attracted to people who fit Kendrick's general description: fair, blue-eyed, trim and compact, exuding an aura of physical competence. In his teens he had dated a few sporty girls, to their mutual disappointment. When he got to university, he finally sorted out that what he was looking for was a *man* who fit that description. Who, in fact, fit the precise description of the young officer sitting directly behind him. It was uncanny, as though his deepest, most secret fantasy had taken shape and walked right into this classroom.

John didn't hear a word the instructor said that day. From the moment his eyes met Kendrick's until the bell rang to signal the end of class, his mind was full of that face—the lean angles of jaw and cheekbones, a squarish chin framing a perfectly shaped mouth, brows like two quick brushstrokes above those extraordinarily blue eyes, and a nose just a little too small for perfect balance that looked as though it might have been broken sometime in the past.

John wasted the government funds being poured into his education as he wondered how a set of relatively ordinary features could fit together to produce perfection. It took all his willpower not to turn around and stare. He was able to control himself only because he knew that if he turned around, he'd have to say something, and if he tried to do that, he would sound like an idiot.

Kevin admitted, later, that he'd been in the same state of numb astonishment, staring at the back of John's head. Neither of them gave the slightest indication of interest, though, not right there in the classroom. Gay men were still extremely circumspect in the British Army—a man's sex life was best kept private if it didn't involve shagging any life-form in a skirt—and in any case, a class on biohazards was hardly a pickup bar.

John was so disconcerted that as soon as class was over, he made a beeline for the men's room and hid in a stall while he summoned his courage to talk to the new student. By the time he came out, Kendrick was nowhere to be seen.

IT WASN'T until later, when John was frowning at the selections in the cafeteria vending machine, that a voice at his elbow said, "You don't want to eat that—it's leftover samples from class. Want to go find some Chinese?"

Kevin could have said, "Want to go find some fried earthworms?" and John would have accepted as promptly. On the way to the Chinese restaurant, he learned that his fantasy man, whose name was Kevin Kendrick, had a voice as low-key and attractive as the rest of him and a comfortable manner that would put anyone at ease. Although Kevin was from a military family, he was by no means certain he wanted to make it his life's work as his father had, but he'd been willing to give it a try. He had only arrived the day before, to take a few specialized courses at this training center.

"And what about you?" Kevin asked. "Why the Army?"

John hadn't really ever been asked that question; the recruiters had been happy enough to have him and were more interested to know that he spoke French and a little German.

"I suppose it sounds a bit antique," John said, "but I thought a few years in the service might teach me something. And it's like jury duty, in a way. Someone has to do it, and if you only leave the dirty work to those too stupid to avoid it, I'm not sure that would leave me feeling all that safe. I've thought about going into police work, eventually—thought the military background would be useful."

"Responsibility," Kevin said. "You don't think it's a dirty word. That's a nice change. Are you an oldest son?"

"Only son," John said. "Only child. My parents died in an accident when I was twelve, and my grandmother raised me the rest of the way. She's gone now, as well."

"I'm sorry."

John shrugged. "Thanks, but that was a long time ago. She was ninety-eight, so it wasn't unexpected."

"No other relatives?"

"Some distant ones somewhere, I think. No one close enough to come to her funeral. I suppose that's another reason the Army looked attractive—I'm not a big joiner, but it's nice to know I belong somewhere. What about your family?"

"The Brigadier—well, that's what we all call my father—he's retired from the Army. My mother has the kind of resourcefulness you'd expect for someone who's raised three kids as a military wife. Older brother, younger sister, various cousins and uncles and aunts. Quite a lot of cousins, enough to spare. Would you like a few?"

"Not until I've met them, but thanks—damn, it's closed!" A sign hung on the locked door of the Chinese takeaway, printed in both English and Chinese. "This happens sometimes," John explained. "Mr. Cheng's an herbalist on the side, and sometimes he just closes the shop for no apparent reason."

Kevin looked up and down the street and spotted the sign over the Indian restaurant a block down. "All right, then. What do you say to Indian?"

"I like it better than Chinese, actually, and Kandahar's quite good. Usually crowded, though—would you mind takeaway?"

Kevin gave him a sidelong glance and a half smile. "I think I'd prefer it."

They wound up taking naan, raita, matar paneer, and curried lamb back to John's flat. The food was excellent, as it always was, and he had no classes until the following afternoon, so there was no time pressure.

The beer helped too, no doubt. But it wasn't only that. John felt comfortable with Kevin, as he seldom had with anyone else, and it seemed to be mutual. Or possibly Kevin was one of those fortunate souls who were naturally gregarious, who could talk with anyone about anything. John found out later that he was only half-right; as a military brat, Kevin had indeed learned to be personable and make friends easily, but not to the degree that they had clicked.

It had been so easy, so natural. They were sitting on the sofa, watching the late sports news—nothing important to either of them—and they talked over the newsreader's monologue. It was the usual caution at first, hints about pubs and films, the little signs and countersigns of establishing gay identity, until Kevin said, quite frankly, "Why don't you just ask? I don't have a girlfriend—have had, but probably won't again. Don't have a boyfriend either."

The unapologetic challenge in those beautiful eyes captured John's heart, then and there. He'd always been shy, never good at quick clever lines, but he heard himself say, "Mind if I apply for the position?"

And Kevin said, grinning, "Which position? Or are you versatile?"

"Side by side," he'd answered, embarrassing himself again.

Kevin's smile lit up the room. "I'd like that."

John smiled back, reached up tentatively to touch Kevin's face, and closed his eyes as Kevin leaned in for a kiss.

It had been like coming home. The taste of his lips, the warmth of that strong, muscled body, even his scent—it all held a faint familiarity, as though this were something they had done many times before. And as the weeks and months passed, it only grew better, unlike John's other—admittedly few—liaisons. The fellow students he'd dated at uni had generally wanted nothing more than no-strings sex, and for John that was a turn-off. The other extreme— the sad but tenacious lad who might have become a stalker if he hadn't been so ineffectual—finally pushed John's patience to the limit, and the breakup had been loud and acrimonious.

Kevin was different. The sex was wonderful, but so was all the time in between. They'd had fun together. Even a simple walk along the shore became something to look forward to. They were both signed up for extended training, so after a couple of weeks Kevin had abandoned his bedsit and moved in, ostensibly to save money. John had become comfortable, had started thinking in terms of settling down.

And then it all went to pieces.

They had not seen each other since the day before John's unit shipped out for Bosnia. And their parting had been—well, not quite what you could call bitter, more bewildered—each of them staring at the other, thinking his lover had gone mad. They had never properly discussed their choices of specialization. They had mentioned possibilities, each had been mildly derisive of the other's ideas, and they'd simply stopped discussing the matter.

That, John knew now, had been the second-worst mistake of his life. His duty choice had been the absolute worst: he had chosen to sign up as a UN peacekeeper, with likely assignment to the Balkans. He was going to prevent war, to protect civilians. The best sort of work for a soldier.

He had been an idealistic fool. So many of them had, even high-ranking officers. How could anyone have foreseen that chaos? The whole society broke down and went back to the Dark Ages. Kosovo. The bloodbath.

He still shied away from thinking about it, for his own sanity's sake. It had been years before the nightmares stopped.

But that choice, naïve though it was, had at least been consistent with John's basic personality. He had gone into the military more out of a desire to protect the helpless than to strut around in a uniform and make guns go bang. Kevin's choice was a total surprise. Calm, brilliant, rational, amiable Kevin had decided to apply for admission to that exclusive crew of trigger-happy, cloak-and-dagger maniacs that called itself the SAS.

If Kevin was still with that mob, he'd have access to all sorts of military information. He would have been able to learn of Lt. John Hanson's nervous breakdown in the midst of that horror in Bosnia. Of his botched suicide, and probably even of the months of medical leave and therapy, and the disability pension, and the fact that he was now back in university, studying psychology in a desperate attempt to find a way to weave his shredded soul back together.

Why would he come to see me now? I must be nine kinds of a security risk! One thing he knew about the SAS—it was one place where sexual orientation was still a major issue.

Which, of course, was why Kevin's decision had come as such a shock. "The SAS," John had joked, when Kevin first told him of his intentions. "Where Men are Men and sheep are scared. You can't be serious—"

"It's *necessary*," Kev had said. His jaw was set, and he was using the voice that said he'd already made up his mind. "Johnny, terrorists are real. Someone has to stop them. It's like what you said the day we met—if everyone backs off because it's a brutal job, then the only ones left to do it are the brutes."

"It's what the job will do to you that worries me. That kind of thing would eat you alive. It's mad."

"No madder than going into a war zone with orders against fighting. It's not as though the UN is taking the Serbs' weapons away, you know." Kevin's fair skin had been flushed with emotion. "You'll be nothing but a helpless observer—there's no peace to keep! That whole operation is a political farce, Johnny—an exercise in military impotence!"

They'd finally realized that no matter how readily they might agree on other things, this was one subject that would always divide them. So they dropped it, made love frantically for the few days they had left, and parted on more or less amiable terms.

The parting of ways didn't change how John felt about Kevin, but time and distance had put an end to the relationship. They had exchanged a couple of brief, superficial e-mails—of course, they had never been indiscreet enough to write anything, anywhere, that might be considered compromising—but there had been so little left to say. *I thought I knew you. I thought I understood you.* Or, more truthfully, *I thought you knew me. I thought you cared enough to stay with me.*

And that brought John back to the mystery of the phone call. Why now, after all these years? What was there left to say?

Or was Kevin waiting for John to say, "You were right"?

No problem there. He *had* been right. Diagnosis: Delayed Stress Syndrome resulting from Military Impotence. *Take two Viagra and a bottle of sleeping pills, call the doctor in the morning if you're still alive.*

Yes, Kev, you were right. And if I know you, you'll say, "I wish I'd been wrong."

John jittered away a quarter of an hour, trying to see the humor in a sitcom that was the least annoying offering, but finally gave up. The sole point seemed to be that no matter how bad your life was, this family was worse, and watching the actors snipe at one another was more painful than amusing. There was a football match on as well, but he could no longer tolerate that fierce conflict over something so meaningless as kicking a ball from one end of a field to the other. Not after watching that same us-and-them intensity turn ordinary men into genocidal monsters.

I liked sports, once.

I used to have a sense of humor.

But something else had not changed at all, despite all that had happened. One thing he had tried to forget that now assumed enormous importance.

I still love him. Want him.

What the hell am I going to do?

He ought to apply himself to his books to pass the time. He'd put that statistics course off as long as he possibly could, but he had to pass it to graduate. And he had to study to pass. And of all the classes he had taken, this was the one he really did not want to take a second time. Study was imperative.

But not tonight. He'd need full concentration to prepare for next week's test, and his mind kept presenting him with distractions. So many years ago, but the memory was so sharp, it could have been last week.

There were other memories along that trail, more recent ones. A woman newly released from hospital, one eye gone, thanking Hanson in broken English for seeing to it that her murdered husband had been buried decently instead of being left to rot in pieces. "He was my life...." The woman wept, holding her surviving child in her arms. "What will I do now?"

Why was she asking him? "Keep going. Keep him alive in your memory. Raise his son to remember his father. Just live one day at a time, what else can you do?"

It was the most honest thing he could have said. It was how he had been surviving, one day after another, ever since Kevin had gone. Whether his words had helped that poor woman, who could say? He had not known the couple at all; he had seen the little family walking past his guard station on their way home every day, and that was all he knew of either of them. He'd been standing there, supposedly guarding the peace, when the Serb truck drove by and gunned down half a dozen innocent civilians. But he wasn't allowed to shoot at them; he was a *Peace*keeper. Armed, dangerous, and hamstrung. All he was allowed to do was bury the victims. He'd given the widow the standard information on refugee assistance, in case she'd wanted to leave, but she told him she had nowhere to go.

He was glad, after he got back to England, that he had at least tried to help her. There had been so little he could do for anyone, to stop the soul-numbing brutality. Serbs returning headless bodies under a flag of truce, then playing football with their victims' heads just over the no-pass line, in full sight of the bereaved families—how could anything have prepared him for that? So many people he'd met, stupid people turned into monsters, decent people trying to make some kind of a life under impossible conditions. So many of them dead now. And here he was, sitting, waiting, afraid to hope—

Even though he'd expected it, the doorbell's ring sent him a foot into the air.

Chapter Two

JOHN GLANCED around the room, noticing the clutter now. He should have tidied up, but there was nothing to be done for it at this point. Same for his loose gray sweatshirt and pants; at least they were clean. He brushed a few biscuit crumbs off the old denim quilt that he kept folded over the back of the futon, shrugged, and clattered down two flights of steps to answer the door.

He opened it without checking and found himself awash in a spicy wave of fragrance, nostalgia, and hunger. A stray thought reminded him that scent-associated memories were very powerful because the olfactory nerve went directly from nose to brain, and he wondered if he'd been studying too much lately.

"I didn't think to ask," Kevin said over an armful of grease-spotted paper bags, "but it occurred to me you might have eaten already and I haven't, so I stopped for a takeaway."

"I haven't," John said, embarrassed at his oversight. "Sorry, Kev, I should have cooked something—"

"There's plenty." Kevin smiled tentatively. "I remember you always get ravenous late at night."

That made him very happy for some reason, and they stood there for a moment, eyes locked, until John realized his bare feet were freezing. "Come on, then!" He shook off the paralysis and reached for the paper bags, noticing Kevin had a blue carryall over his left shoulder. His heart took a leap. He turned to the stairway to cover his emotions. "I'm at the top, penthouse level. Lots of healthful exercise and cheap rent." He could hear his heart pounding as they ascended the stairs, but not from exercise. "So how've you been?"

No reply. Maybe he hadn't heard. Kevin followed him up to the flat, stepped inside, and stood quietly as John locked the door, then trailed along to the tiny kitchenette and took the covered foil tins out of the bag while John fetched plates from the cabinet.

"Coat hook's behind the door," John said over his shoulder.

Kevin hung his jacket, dropped his canvas bag beneath it, and said, without preamble, "You were right, Johnny."

John nearly dropped the crockery. "What?"

"You were right. About the SAS."

"I'm sorry." He set the plates down and said the only thing he could. "Well, you were right too."

Kevin made a choked sound that must have been meant as a laugh. "For a couple of smart officers who were both right, we made quite a balls-up, didn't we?"

He looked at Kevin then, really looked, and saw how tightly wound his friend was. Saw the pain. Easy enough to recognize that, yes, indeed. "What happened, Kev? I don't understand."

Kevin was incredulous. "You don't? What, haven't you watched the news in the last couple of weeks? Read about the Court of Inquiry?"

"Court—my God—you?" He could not imagine Kevin doing anything so dreadful that he would be subjected to something like that. "No, I haven't. Nothing."

"You're serious?"

John swallowed. It hadn't taken long to get to this point. He had hoped they might at least have a little while together before he was forced to give up what had been and reveal his lovely new flaws. "No. I—I mean, yes, I'm serious, and no, I almost never watch the news anymore. And I don't read much of the paper. I'm a refugee from the information age." That earned him a slight grin, so he explained. "I had a choice: give up beer for Prozac, or give up the nightly news and keep the beer. I don't much miss the news."

Kevin stared at him disbelievingly, and then the lines of strain on his face shifted. A snicker escaped. "Really?"

"It's not funny!"

"I'm... I'm not laughing." But he was. "Christ, Johnny, that's brilliant! Wish I'd thought of it!" He sobered almost immediately. "Wouldn't have done much good, though...."

John wasn't quite sure what to say. "Well, that food smells good—be a shame to let it get cold. Let's eat now. You can tell me what happened later, if you want to."

"I suppose I'll have to. One good thing about a media disaster, I don't have to keep you in the dark. I don't think anyone's resigned so publicly since Edward traded his crown for Wallis Simpson. But you're right; the whole story may sit better on a full stomach."

"Beer?" Decent beer was his one indulgence, and he had a couple weeks' worth in the cabinet.

"Yes. I could use it." Kevin's mouth tightened, not quite a smile. "I've made it a point not to drink alone, right now. Too easy to slide over the edge."

John wanted to ask what had happened but realized he would get the answer eventually. So he pulled out two bottles and asked, "What did you get for us?"

"Bread, mixed veg curry, saag paneer, and some chicken tikka for you."

He laughed. "What, you've gone veggie on me?"

Kevin bit his lip. "On our last action, we had casualties. Two of my men were killed. I stood there staring at the bodies—couldn't believe they were dead, you know?" He closed his eyes briefly. "Stupid, isn't it? The next time I sat down and ordered chops, I took one look and ran for the loo, heaved my boots up. It's nothing to do with the animal; I just keep seeing them lying there, dead. Just... meat."

"Ah, love—" Half his mind was screaming to stop before he ruined everything, but he couldn't. It was only a step across the little space, and then he had Kevin in his arms, holding him as a floodgate of tears burst loose. So strange—how long had it been since he'd been the one weeping out the horrors? "It's all right, Kev, don't worry, it's just me, you can't possibly be more fucked-up than I've been."

Arms snaked around his ribs, Kevin hanging on for dear life. John leaned back against the cooker, holding him, drinking in the closeness but damning the cause. "One of my men—when we got back—same thing. He couldn't even defrost a chop. It's nothing wrong with you, it's just sensory overload. It eases, in time...."

"Sorry," Kevin mumbled against his neck. "Didn't mean to—"

"It's all right," he said again. "I know what you mean. It's the blood. The smell. Gets into your nose...." Odd, now that he thought of it. When he ate meat himself, he always made certain it was cooked through. And spicy, loaded down with any sort of sauce. It didn't have that rank, dead smell when it was spicy.

"Well." Kevin's arms fell away, and he straightened. "I didn't realize—sorry. Blood sugar's down, I think. Haven't eaten all day. I had to go and clear out my office, and I didn't see any point in embarrassing myself further." Even now, Kevin didn't look like a man walking the razor's edge. As always, he was impeccable: a tailored shirt open at the collar, V-neck cashmere sweater, well-pressed trousers, and sports jacket. He could have just stepped out of a faculty lounge or off the pages of a gentlemen's magazine. But the pain was there in his eyes, in the tightness of his mouth.

"Sit down, then." John put a bottle in his hand and pointed to the futon. "I'll dish this up."

Kevin had finished the beer before John got the plates filled. He'd found a set of four folding trays at a thrift shop, though this was the first occasion he'd had to use more than one of them. He balanced both plates on one tray and dropped the second onto his friend's knees, sliding Kevin's plate down when the tray stopped joggling. "Here. Get some of this into you. I'll get you another bottle."

"'Malt,'" Kevin said, "'does more than Milton can, to justify God's ways to man.'"

"Glad to hear it." He put the food and beer carton on a third tray and settled himself on the futon with everything in easy reach. If Kevin needed to get drunk, this was the safest time and place he could find. *Safe from the world?* a mocking voice in his head inquired. *Or safe from you?*

I'm not going to hurt him. Of that he was sure. But how could he judge? Here he was, still trying to get himself back to something approaching normal, presuming to know what was best for his dearest friend and erstwhile lover. Yes, he wanted to take Kevin in his arms, take him to bed, reach back to that time before they were both so badly damaged. But his own motives should be examined. The ethical injunction against treating one's own family had a sound basis.

Then again, if Kevin had wanted an Army psych doc, he would surely have had access to one. The SAS might even have insisted on it. *But he came here instead. Or maybe after they were through with him.*

He came back to me. The thought simultaneously warmed and frightened him, and he set it aside for a little while to enjoy the Indian food. Interesting that Kevin had chosen this echo of their first time, the same sort of food but not the same selections. He had brought all John's favorites too. He'd remembered.

They both ate ravenously and finished off a few more beers. "I forgot dessert," Kevin said at last.

"Too full right now." John set the tray down beside his feet. "There might be ice cream in the freezer."

"You're right. Maybe later." Kevin relaxed against the cushions, staring upward. "D'you know there's a spider on your ceiling?"

"Good. It'll keep the flies away." He leaned back too, suddenly aware of how close Kevin was. He could smell Kevin's aftershave, something new that blended deliciously with the food's aromas, could hear the faint exhalation of his breath, even sense the warmth rising off his body. He turned slightly, just to look at him, and saw that Kevin was watching him too.

"Your hair's longer." Kevin touched John's short pigtail. "I like it, but—?"

"I didn't want to look like a soldier anymore. Saves on haircuts too—I can trim the front myself." He ran his fingers through Kevin's shorter military cut. His hair looked nearly brown now, not the dark blond it had been years back. "You need to get out in the sun more often."

"I suppose I do. This past year...." He sighed. "It's been like living under a rock."

"And I don't suppose you're allowed to talk about it."

"Not much, no. This last mess—yes, some of it. But not right now."

The expression in his eyes said well enough what he'd like to do now; it didn't need to be spoken. They slowly leaned in toward one another, but John's scruples got the better of him, and he put a hand on Kevin's cheek. "Kev, not that I don't want to—but are you sure?"

In answer Kevin seized him by the hair and devoured his mouth. Right or wrong, he was sure. And John had never been more certain of anything in his life. *He's using you,* that nasty little voice in his head told him smugly. *He wants to feel alive, and he knows you'll do that for him.*

Yes, he acknowledged. *I suppose he does. And if I can, I will! And what's wrong with that?* A fierce resentment at the whole notion of clinical detachment flashed through him, and he let Kevin's need pull him out of his intellect and back into his body. How long had it been? Too long. Years. It was all very well for a psychiatrist to tell him he needed to work on his own emotions first, but unless you had someone else to exercise those emotions with, what was the point?

And it was so sweet, better than his favorite memories. There was nothing in the world to match the taste of Kevin's mouth. He ran his hands up under Kevin's sweater, tugged the tail of his shirt free so he could slide his hand in to stroke that sensitive spot at the base of Kevin's spine. Kev shivered, and the two of them started to slide sideways. Then Kevin let out a yelp.

"What's wrong?" John gasped, untangling himself.

Halfway on top of him, Kevin shifted his weight. "Right arm. I've got to be careful. Don't worry, it's almost healed."

Our last action. We had casualties.... John's blood turned to ice water. "My God, *you were shot?*" His hand shook as he reached to touch the sleeve. "How? When?"

"Tell you later. Not now, Johnny, please...." Kevin grabbed John's sweatshirt with both hands, demonstrating that he could use the arm. It was not terribly obvious that the right arm didn't move quite as easily as the left, and John pretended not to notice, shivering as the cool air hit his bare skin. "It's nearly well," Kevin said. "Just don't flop over on it."

The hem of the shirt caught John's chin; while he was untangling himself, Kevin took advantage of the distraction, pushing him flat and lunging on top of him like he was going for a goal, nuzzling hungrily at the juncture of neck and shoulder, and John had to laugh. "Kevin, if you want something, just ask."

Pulling a cushion under his own head, he held Kevin close, careful this time to let that right arm dangle over the edge. He'd been surprised, their first time together, at how strong Kevin was despite the difference in their height. He wasn't surprised now, just relieved that Kevin seemed his old eager self. Whatever else had befallen them, that at least had not changed.

He stopped trying to think and just let himself feel—the warm mouth and cool breath on his throat sending shivers down his spine, the soft brush of the sweater on his belly, the hardness against his thigh. It was happening faster than he expected, faster than he'd hoped, maybe faster than he wanted—but he would have died sooner than stop it.

Kevin's mouth slid up the side of his jaw; their lips met again, and he was overwhelmed, wrapping his arms and legs around Kev, hardly believing it was real but determined to hold on. He should get his pants off, he should get Kevin out of those clothes, they really should—and what about a condom?—but it was too late, he had Kev's arse in both hands, and they were rocking together, lunging against each other. Release swept over him in a rush, Kevin cried out, and for a little while, it felt as though they'd melted into a single heap of warm flesh and rumpled clothing.

"My God, that was...." Kevin started to raise his head, then sighed and relaxed again. Another deep breath, and the tension left his body altogether. He'd gone to sleep! John grinned and buried his nose in the cowlick at the crown of Kevin's head. Kev smelled so good. He always managed to smell good, even marinated in curry powder and Newcastle Brown Ale. It was ridiculous, but such a lovely thing to fall asleep this way.

Chapter Three

THE COMPOUND. Firefight. His men are trapped, enemies all around, and he can't get to them, can't even make himself heard over the thunder of automatic weapons. He feels the slug slam into him, his arm dropping uselessly to his side, numb for a little while and then throbbing. He stumbles, the side of his head slams into the wall, and he finds himself fading in and out of consciousness, lying dazed with his face against the cold concrete, waiting for the next bullet. The last one.

Then the firing stops, and the quiet is worse. As his ears clear, he hears gasping, cursing, moans—and sirens in the distance. One ordeal is over, a worse one just beginning.

He moves among the casualties like a sleepwalker. All his men. All his men, dead or dying. And off to one side, another body, not one of his squad. A tall man, slim, his wiry build and untidy dark hair terribly familiar.

Heart in his mouth, he moves toward this body, kneels to turn it over.

"Don't bother with that," someone orders from behind him. "It's nothing important, just dead meat."

He reaches down anyway with his left arm and somehow levers the body over so he can meet the accusation in Johnny's dead, unfocused eyes.

Kevin jerked awake and found that same face an inch away from his own, long dark lashes resting like closed window shades against his skin. But they were lying on a hard-cushioned futon, not concrete, and John was merely sleeping—sleeping deeply and apparently comfortably despite the eleven stone draped across him.

"Johnny?" Kevin asked tentatively. When he got no response apart from a slight snore, he extricated himself and got to his feet. John seemed to be profoundly unconscious, his arms limp as bags of sand when Kevin rearranged him in what looked like a more comfortable position.

John was such a beautiful thing to look at asleep, his quicksilver energy at rest like a hummingbird perched on a wire. The sharp planes of his face were an arresting contrast to those lush, incredibly soft lips, and even though he was self-conscious about his nose, it was in perfect balance with the rest of his features. And his throat—what was it about that long clean curve that was so irresistible? Maybe it was knowing how sensitive it was, how Johnny trembled and gasped when Kevin kissed him there. Perhaps that was the answer; the landscape of his body was not only beautiful in itself, but a reminder of all the pleasure given and shared. It was arousing just to stand and drink in the sight, something he thought he'd never see again.

But John must be getting cold by now, half-naked as he was, no matter how fine a sight he made. Kevin sighed and pulled the blue patchwork quilt off the high back of the futon and tucked it around his sleeping lover.

He took a step back and nearly tripped over the dinner trays. Neat by nature as well as years of military discipline, he collected the clutter, saved what little was left of the food, and put it into the fridge.

He had to smile. How could Johnny have said anything about making dinner? There was nothing in there but a pint of milk, a leg of roast chicken in barbecue sauce, half a bag of carrots, and something gruesome in a jar. He'd have to take Johnny out for breakfast. That would be lovely, just like old times. He consigned the rest of the rubbish to the bin, put the empty bottles into their carton, then washed the plates and set them to dry.

All that, and John was still snug in the arms of Morpheus. *I wonder if he always sleeps that soundly? Hope so.* Kevin himself still could not sleep through the night. It had been worse immediately after the disaster, when he was hospitalized for the concussion and gunshot wound. Even after he was released, it had been nearly impossible for him to fall asleep. The pain pills had helped a little—and he'd needed them—but the sleep they induced was as satisfying as eating cardboard for bread, and it seemed they made the nightmares worse, like opening a door on hell. He'd stopped using the pills as soon as he could; he was not going to give away any more of himself, especially to something that would certainly rot what was left of his life.

And what, exactly, *was* left of his life? He'd had a few weeks to think about that while his arm healed and his career crumbled. He flexed his right hand, trying to determine whether those two numb fingers were any better. The nerve would regenerate eventually, or so the physiotherapist said, but he couldn't feel any difference yet.

He glanced at the clock in the little galley kitchen. He'd arrived at ten minutes to eight; they'd eaten at about quarter past, been asleep by nine… and it was now going on eleven, and John was still dead to the world. A shower together would have been nice, but if Kevin left his underwear on any longer, he'd need industrial solvents to get himself out of them.

Decision made, he did a quick reconnaissance and located the bath—a shower stall, really—and scrubbed himself clean. A freshly laundered pair of sweatpants hung from a towel hook; apparently this was John's new uniform. Kevin decided he'd have to borrow them for the time being and rinse out his trousers later. At least he'd let himself hope enough to bring a change of socks and underwear.

He padded back out to the living room and found the situation much as it had been, the only difference being that John had rolled onto his side. Kevin decided to give him another half hour and then roust him out. The double bed in the back room looked considerably more comfortable, and he really did not want to sleep alone tonight.

He found himself studying John's new home, trying to read it for information about its inhabitant. The main room, like the flat itself, was smallish but practical, separated from the kitchen area by a waist-level countertop. The living room floor was covered by a tract of generic beige carpet, and the kitchen had equally nondescript white vinyl tiles. A couple of good-sized windows filled most of the wall opposite the kitchen, and the sofa sat at the end nearer the door, facing a very small television. Only one object hung on a wall beside the door: a framed poster of a woodland scene that Johnny had bought from a street vendor not long after they'd first met. John had sworn it was a landscape of Middle-earth; the fellow selling it had no idea where the picture was taken but was happy to agree it might be Rivendell when he saw the £5 note offered without haggling.

That picture was the only physical object Kevin remembered from John's previous flat, apart from his bed and a chest of drawers, and its presence was indefinably reassuring. Whatever had driven John to the point of suicide, there was still that core of imagination that could send deep roots into an ancient forest of fantasy. When he'd eventually been nagged into reading the books, Kevin had pictured his lover first as Frodo, then later as Aragorn, though he'd never told him so. He'd enjoyed the films and wondered what John thought of them. He didn't see a DVD player; when he cleared out his quarters, he could bring his over. Maybe they could make popcorn and have a Middle-earth marathon.

Would Johnny let him stay on for a few days? Probably so. Despite all the time they'd been apart, their bodies hadn't forgotten, and the one issue that had come between them no longer existed. But it would be unfair and unreasonable to ask for more than a few days. Even if they could recapture what they'd lost, he had to give Johnny time to decide whether he wanted to try.

But this was a comfortable place, even though it was small. John had put long, low bookshelves along the whole wall beneath the windows. They looked like something he might have built himself, and, of course, there was his battered set of the Tolkien trilogy, now almost completely surrounded by popular and scholarly books on psychology. At the far corner of the room, between the television and the windows, sat a two-disc compact CD player, the kind Kevin had had at university, complete with headphones. An old but comfortable-looking recliner stood beside it, a floor lamp next to that. The stack of textbooks and a bulging backpack revealed that John was taking three courses this term.

Kevin settled into the chair and donned the headset. He pushed away the sudden pang of loss; he would never be wearing one of these on a mission again, coordinating his men on a life-and-death assignment. He was curious to hear what John had in the machine after all this time. Johnny always had an eclectic taste in music—the current interest could be anything from Debussy to Top 40 to Ladysmith Black Mambazo—though unless he had changed a lot, his current tunes would not be anything sung by men in cowboy hats or gangstas in baggy pants. John was intermittently musical, too. He would play a favorite disc until he'd memorized it—and until Kevin was ready to break it to pieces—then let the stereo gather dust for a week or two. It would have made more sense if John actually played an instrument, but he never had.

The music that hit his ears was unexpected. A hard, driving beat, a woman's husky voice accusing her lover of running to another out of fear. It was damned uncanny. Had John set this up for him to hear? He'd had time to do it, but it was completely unlike him. The singer was still accusing, asserting that she was the only one who would go through hell for this wandering wretch.

And how would Johnny have known about that little misadventure? Coincidence. It had to be.

Kevin chuckled when the song suggested the singer's lover break in through a window and wait for her to come home. Yes, that sounded like a proper SAS courtship. He could have tried that approach too, if he'd wanted to scare Johnny into cardiac arrest.

He found the CD case and belatedly recognized the artist as the American singer Melissa Etheridge. He vaguely remembered having read that she was a lesbian. Interesting how it changed things to imagine that she was singing to another woman rather than a man. Scanning the printed lyrics, he found one song—the one he was hearing now—making the discouraging statement that there were some bridges burned beyond repair. He hoped that was not a message—the warm welcome he'd been given made that unlikely.

Kevin, old man, you have spent far too long in the cloak-and-dagger business. John Hanson bought music because he liked it. He would never have sought out a CD—a secondhand one at that, judging from the sticker—on the remote chance that an old lover whom he had not seen in years would drop by and scan it for obscure messages. The choice of music was, in all likelihood, due simply to the fact that John enjoyed it. It was interesting music, performed with skill. That was all he usually asked for.

And then Kevin heard the chorus of that song, as Etheridge proclaimed that she would face fear and pain to identify demons of the past and dispel them, that the ordeal must be endured in order to heal. Yes, there was a message there, but it was not directed to anyone else, and he suddenly felt embarrassed at the uninvited glimpse into his lover's soul. He hit the Stop button and switched to the other disc.

It was a rich male voice this time, an operatic tenor, but not opera music. He found the case: Bocelli, *Romanza*, and most of the lyrics were in Italian, so Kevin simply leaned back to enjoy the music, passionate but somehow soothing, devoid of hidden meanings.

He must have dozed. He jerked as fingers brushed his cheek but managed to bring himself awake before he did anything dangerous.

"It's midnight," John said, leaning down to kiss him. "Ready for bed?"

Johnny looked too sleepy to be generating double entendres, but the question was so loaded that Kevin just nodded. "I thought you might be out for the night." He noticed that the futon had not been opened into a bed and decided to avoid ambiguity. "Given what we did after dinner, this is probably a stupid question, but where would you like me to sleep?"

John blinked. "With me. Of course. Unless you'd rather not." Standing there barefooted and sleepy, stained sweatpants sliding down his hips, he looked like a child who'd just lost his puppy. "Sorry, Kev, I only thought—"

"No, no," Kevin assured him, climbing out of the chair. "That's fine." He put his hands on John's smooth shoulders, stroking him like a nervy colt. "I hoped that was what you meant. I only wanted to be sure. When I called earlier, I didn't know if you'd even want to see me. It's been a long time, and I thought you might've found someone else."

Johnny pulled him close, then, after a long embrace, eased back enough to look at him solemnly. "I don't believe there will ever be anyone else," he said. "Not like you, not for me." He yawned. "Kev, I think we have to talk, but I'm 'shagged out followin' a prolonged squawk.' Can we sleep on it?"

Kevin blinked at the Monty Python quote, but recognized the good sense of John's suggestion and was very grateful for such a sane, reasonable proposition. "Of course. Just throw a pillow over me if I get noisy. I've been having dreams…."

John nodded. "I can imagine. There might be something we can do to help with that—no, not drugs, I'll explain in the morning." He slid a hand down to Kevin's rump. "You didn't waste any time getting into my pants!"

Kevin fell back into their old banter without a second thought. "You want me out of 'em?"

"In the morning. Right now I couldn't keep my eyes open, no fault of yours."

With one of John's arms serving as a pillow and the other wrapped around his shoulders, Kevin found he had no difficulty getting back to sleep.

KEVIN WOKE sitting bolt upright, gasping, his heart pounding, wanting to scream his terror at the abyss of loneliness yawning before him. The details of the dream that woke him were gone. Only the panic remained. His hand went out instinctively; the touch of the warm body beside him helped, but he had to wait, to feel that naked chest move with an indrawn breath.

When Johnny muttered and moved closer, the cold knot in his belly loosened. A dream. Just a dream. The room was quiet, moonlight spilling through the open window, nothing moving but the tracery of tree branches against the duvet.

An army of lovers cannot fail? Maybe not. But I doubt if they rest easy.

He settled back down and tried to sleep, but oblivion was a long time coming.

Chapter Four

"JOHNNY?"

John thought he'd been having a beautiful dream until he swam up to awareness and realized there truly was a hand on his shoulder. "You're really here," he said, and opened his eyes.

"Yes." Kevin must have been up for a while already; he'd shaved, but wore only a pair of white briefs. "I made tea, it's in the kitchen. What would you like to do?"

"Persuade you to take those off," John said, raising an eyebrow at the underwear.

Kevin's smile told him he'd got the answer right, and he smiled back, then found himself at a painfully awkward impasse. They had both been scrupulously careful when they'd been together, and honest with one another. Life and death were things neither of them took lightly. "Kev, I hate to ask... and as far as I'm concerned, it isn't necessary—" *Damn!*

"What?"

He pushed himself up to a sitting position. "Hell of a question, I'm sorry, but—do we need condoms?"

Kevin started to say something, then took a deep breath. "No. I didn't need a transfusion, and they ran the whole battery of tests when I was patched up. You've been getting tested?"

"No. No need."

"Seven *years*?"

The incredulity in Kevin's voice felt almost like an accusation, and John knew his face must have shown his embarrassment.

"Johnny, I'm sorry—I only meant, how could you go that long without anybody falling in love with you? You're so—" He shook his head helplessly.

So totally fucked-up only a pervert would have wanted me, John finished mentally, and forced a smile. "I'm not outgoing like you are, Kev. I was never voted 'most popular.' And there just hasn't been anyone worth the effort. How about you?"

Kevin flushed. "Just one. After you, it was hard to find anyone who measured up. But I took precautions. Without protection, she would never have—"

"*She?*" He didn't mean it to sound accusing either; he was just surprised.

Kevin turned even redder, then shrugged. "Yes. Trying to see if it was something I could change, I suppose. It wasn't."

John understood without having to think much about it. "You needed to fit in with the group."

"I—I suppose so." He looked down, then took a step back, his voice and body tightening. "I'm sorry, Johnny. I didn't mean to interfere with your life. I'll leave, if you want. I'm sorry."

"No!" John was out of the bed, standing in the doorway before Kevin could get through it, terrified he'd just ruined everything. "No, it's all right—I didn't expect you'd been a monk, but I wanted to know if it was safe—or to give you the chance to protect yourself if you weren't sure of me. I don't want to use 'em unless we have to."

He could see the emotions shifting on Kevin's face almost faster than he could name them; John had always loved the man's openness, but it was clear that Kevin's time with the SAS had made him much more guarded. That was reasonable; he'd had everything to lose from a careless word. *While I have everything to lose if I don't speak up.*

"Kev, it's only me. I love you, I want you, I want you to stay—and I need to know what you want. This isn't a debriefing." Embarrassed at his own babbling, he gave Kev's waistband a playful snap. "Though it could be."

Kevin sighed; his shoulders relaxed a little. "This wasn't what I intended, Johnny." He gave a pained half smile, went back to bed, and flopped down on the pillow. "I really hadn't planned to be such a basket case."

John let himself breathe again. "You're not. If you'd seen me a few years ago…. Give me two minutes, would you? All that beer." He made a temporary retreat to the loo, wondering whether Kevin would be willing to talk. He'd managed to avoid it pretty neatly so far, but they really did need to figure out what they wanted, what they were expecting of one another. It looked as though he'd have to be the one to ask, and he'd somehow have to manage it without making Kev feel as though he was being interrogated. One wrong step, and he could lose the most precious thing in his life, just when he'd got it back against all hope and reason.

I'm not ready for this.

But life didn't wait until you were ready, did it? Besides, there wasn't anybody else. He had to do what he could, because he had a queasy feeling that if he missed this second chance, Kevin would disappear again, this time for good.

Kevin had always been something of a perfectionist, an unusual one in that he didn't expect perfection of anyone else. But the standard he set for himself was always very, very high. John had never doubted Kevin would qualify for the SAS, no matter how demanding the requirements might have been. He'd heard the usual rumors—that candidates had to walk naked through a trench of bloody entrails, that they were beaten, starved, half-killed with exposure. He suspected most of the rumors had some basis in fact. Every warrior elite had its own initiation ordeals.

Of course, Kevin had passed them, and being who he was, he would never have made much of his accomplishment. But somehow, in the line of duty, he had failed—failed very badly and very publicly. That must have been devastating. Whether he was ready to talk about it was another matter, and for the first time in ages, John nearly regretted that he had stopped watching the evening news. Nearly. He'd always hoped to see Kevin again, but he was happier that it had been at his door, not as the target of some acid-tongued news "personality."

He took the quick shower he'd been too groggy for the previous night and returned to the bedroom to find Kevin asleep again, one arm thrown across the pillow beside him. The sun had risen high enough to send a few rays through the east window, and Kev was right in the middle of the light, curled up like a cat. He looked so vulnerable, so young, despite the fact that they'd both be turning thirty this year.

John draped his towel over the doorknob, climbed into bed, and took Kevin in his arms. The shift in his breathing said he was awake now, and waiting.

"I'm glad you came here," John said finally. "Whatever's happened, whatever's going to happen—thank you for coming back."

"I'm sorry I took so long, Johnny." The words were quiet, mumbled against his skin. "I should have been there for you when you got home."

The memories from that wretched time were mercifully fuzzy now. He had thought about Kevin back then, often, but had never had the energy to do anything about finding him. "I didn't try to find you either. I suppose I could have at least tried." He sighed. "It's just as well. I wasn't fit to be with anyone."

"Thought you must've found someone else. I tried, not quite two years ago. To see how you were, tell you I was in line for a command. It was carefully hinted that you had become a potential security risk. I should have told them to stuff it. Instead, I backed down."

"I was a risk, though. I expect I still am. Will your being here now create problems?"

"Johnny, I don't care anymore. But no, I don't think so. I'm not the valuable commodity I once was. Or maybe it's the new military gay policies and the civil rights laws. At any rate, I told them straight out if my friendship with you would put me completely out of the picture, they might as well shoot me then and there."

"*What?*"

"Figuratively speaking." Kevin pulled away a little. "You really don't know about it."

John shook his head.

"Oh, damn."

For all his good intentions just a few minutes earlier, John suddenly did not want Kevin to explain what had happened. Not in his current mood, not if it had to start with him apologizing for things he had done, or not done, years earlier. "You don't have to tell me about it right now."

Kev's jaw was set. "It won't get any easier."

John ran a hand down Kevin's chest to the underwear spoiling his view. "I was hoping it would get harder." And sure enough, it did, pushing back against the pressure of his hand. He tried a kiss and felt Kev's mouth relax beneath his. "Can the news of the world wait for a little while?"

"How long did you say it's been?" Kevin reached down too, caressing John's fast-growing erection with a speculative frown. "I don't know if I can handle seven years' backlog before breakfast," he warned.

"Let's just go for a week's worth. Raise up." He slipped the briefs down Kevin's legs, marveling at that trim, masculine body— strong shoulders, beautifully muscled limbs, strong but not overdeveloped, neither too much nor too little body hair. If he were set to design a picture of male perfection, he could not improve on what lay before him now. The beauty of it took his breath away. "Jesus, Kev," he said. He let his fingers drift through a sprinkling of chest hair that looked like pure gold where the morning sun touched it, and tried not to notice the little scars that hadn't been there before. "I don't know where to start. No, maybe I do. I've learned a thing or two since the last time."

"I thought you said you hadn't—"

"I learned something that is *almost* better than sex. Roll over."

"That doesn't sound like 'almost,'" Kevin said, but he did as John asked, plumping a pillow under his face and glancing back over his shoulder. It was, as John's grandmother had once said in reference to something else, a picture no artist could paint.

John sighed. "I will never get tired of looking at your arse."

"Flattery will get you somewhere, but it's not better—*oh!*"

John had settled one hand on each cheek and begun to slowly rotate them, pressing lightly with his palms. "For a while," he said, "quite a long while, I was so dissociated I hardly realized I had a body." He glanced around the room and located what he was looking for over on the storage chest. "Stay put."

"That was nice, but—"

"I'm not finished." He found the bottle of sandalwood-scented oil he'd bought ages ago, poured a little in his palms, and rubbed them together as he settled himself between Kevin's legs. He reached up to Kev's shoulders, spreading the oil down, pausing for a deep breath of the intoxicating combination of scents, especially the part that was clean, healthy male—the man he had never thought to see again, to lie with again. He was astonished at his own sudden lust. He had gone without for so long that his body had gone into sexual hibernation, but right at this moment, he only wanted to throw himself on this beautiful man and fuck them both into a stupor.

And if he touched Kev's arse right now, he would do just that. *Slow the hell down!* he told himself sternly.

Taking a deep breath, he started at Kevin's heels, kneading the soles of the feet with his thumbs. Kevin groaned.

"Does that hurt?"

"Are you crazy? It's wonderful, don't stop!"

He grinned and continued kneading. His hands were big enough that he could use one on each calf. It wasn't the most professional massage in the world, but he was willing to bet it was the first one Kevin had ever experienced. "I was like a rock," he said. "Didn't even realize it. My therapist told me to go get a massage and recommended someone."

Kevin was hardly paying attention. "Ummm."

He had to use both hands on each strong thigh, working the muscles away from the bone as Pat had taught him. "It took me weeks to get up the nerve to let anyone touch me, but when I finally did, it felt so good I thought for a while about studying physiotherapy. Might still do that. There are some branches of therapy, body-mind techniques…." He'd got back to Kevin's bum and let himself play a little, letting one oiled finger slide between the cheeks, slipping just far enough in to tease, eliciting a moan and a delicious shiver. Not the sort of thing one would ever do to an actual patient—totally unethical in what Pat called the "therapeutic context," but she had once suggested that massaging a lover was something else altogether… and much more fun.

She was right.

"Oh, Christ, Johnny…. How'd you learn this? Should I be jealous?"

"No. The doctor sent me to an actual medical massage person. A lesbian."

Kevin chuckled. "Clever. *Oh*—yeah, do that again...."

He obliged. "Very clever. Safe, sympathetic—but no threat, no temptation, and not likely to let me pull anything if I *had* been tempted. Good thing she doesn't look like you." He straddled Kev's thighs, enjoying the feel of warm bare skin beneath him, and dug his thumbs gently into the lines of muscles along the spine. "You are the most beautiful human being I have ever seen."

"You're mistaken, you know."

"Not from where I sit." He leaned forward a little, letting his cock rest along the cleft of that perfect arse. "By the time we get out of this bed, we'll have to send out for pizza."

"Mmm," Kevin said once more. "I suppose I'm in no position to argue."

"No. But I'm not about to criticize your position. Arguing wasn't what I had in mind." He put a little more oil on his hands, stroked it across those smooth golden shoulders, and had to stop for a breath to get himself under control. He couldn't very well just start humping; this was supposed to be a slow, gentle seduction. Not that Kevin really required seducing. With the way he was writhing under John's ministrations, he was well beyond the need for any persuasion.

"Are you going to do something soon," Kevin inquired, his voice a bit hoarse, "or am I supposed to just lie here and explode?"

If he were doing this with serious therapeutic intent, the next thing would be to work on Kevin's arms. But he didn't want to do that, particularly not until he learned the story behind the uneven red mark on the back of the right triceps, a mark he recognized as a partially healed exit wound. He didn't even want to look at it; he certainly didn't much like thinking about where it had come from. At least it was only an arm—not an eye, not his face, not some vital organ. It was a wound from which Kevin could recover.

John shivered and leaned down to kiss Kevin on the nape of his neck, rubbing his lips through the short stiff hair of the military trim. He nuzzled around to one side, licked the back of Kevin's ear, and grinned as a shiver went through him. "Are you ready?"

"I've *been* ready," Kevin said plaintively. "If you don't do something soon, I'm going to start without you!"

"Which way?"

Kevin shoved his rump up and back, and John carefully lubricated himself and Kevin with more oil.

"Been awhile?"

"Same as you. Come *on*, Johnny...."

"No, we did quick and dirty last night. It'll go too fast no matter what...." Slowly, with infinite care, he positioned himself and pressed forward. Slow. Careful. He would rather cut off his own arm than hurt Kev through impatience, but Kevin's soft cries were not from pain, and he was pushing back with his usual determination.

And then John was fully inside, and they were both breathing hard, half crying, and instinct took over. The years dissolved, time and distance and disappointment and longing banished in the immediacy of the moment. The tension gathered inside him as he thrust into the welcoming body, excitement building until he simply couldn't be careful. He tugged Kevin's hips up, reaching under to bring him along, holding him close with his other arm across his lover's chest. As he pumped with one hand, he had that odd illusion that it was his own cock he was holding, as his whole body quivered on the edge of climax—and then Kev cried out and shuddered, squeezing tight, and it was like setting off a string of firecrackers one right after another. He thrust, and thrust again, and then they both dropped onto the mattress, panting.

They rolled to one side, Kevin curled in his embrace.

"You all right?" John asked after a minute.

"Better than." He let out a huge sigh. "Johnny."

"What?"

"If you decide to do *that* for a living...."

John laughed. "Only for a very select clientele."

"How select?"

"You."

"Good."

They lay there for a while, catching their breath, and John realized that, for the first time in longer than he could remember, he was happy. Simply happy. He kissed the top of Kevin's head and relaxed, enjoying the novelty of it.

In a very little while, Kevin cleared his throat. "Johnny?"

"Mm?"

"Do you have anything in this place that's fit to eat, or would you like to go to breakfast?"

"Whatever you like."

"Mm. Maybe a nap first."

"Sounds fine."

Chapter Five

THE SUN had shifted to the southern window by the time they awoke, and the pot of tea Kevin had left to brew was stone-cold and strong enough to strip paint. He raised an eyebrow when John poured some into a mug and stuck it in the microwave.

"There's an American in one of my study groups," John said when he caught Kevin's expression. "We sometimes meet here. One afternoon I started to pour out half a cold pot, and she said, 'Why waste it?' and I couldn't think of any reason. Apparently Yanks can't taste the difference. Don't worry, we'll get a fresh pot with breakfast."

Kevin wasn't going to argue—he'd used the last of the teabags anyway. He *could* taste the difference, but it cleared away the cobwebs, and the milk took the edge off. "Damn!" He set his mug down as his brain, sluggish after finally having gotten enough sleep, reminded him of a waiting pile of laundry. "We can't go anywhere decent, Johnny—I'll have to borrow your sweats again until I can wash my things."

"Jeans will do," John said. "I've got some you can wear."

"I'll have to roll them up—I'll look a fool."

"No, you won't—come on, I think I know where they are." He rummaged under the bed and retrieved a plastic storage box, then pulled out a pair of folded jeans. "Here," he said, tossing them up to Kevin. "Those should fit."

The jeans were too short for John's long legs, but they were not new and looked vaguely familiar.

As well they should. They were his own.

Ah, Johnny.... He bit his lip. "You kept them? All this time?"

"I kept meaning to give them to Oxfam or something, but... I thought I might see you again, sooner or later, and I could give them back." He shrugged, with a slightly guilty grin. "That's the half-truth. The whole truth is that I just didn't want to let go of them. They were all I had left of you."

Kevin didn't know what to say. He had spent the last year or so in an odd kind of isolation, feeling that there had been no one who could possibly understand the tightrope he was walking, no one who would care. And all that time there had been someone waiting, someone he had deliberately turned his back on to chase a prize that had crumbled to dust just as he'd grasped it.

He finally looked up and met warm dark eyes. "I've been a fool."

"Welcome to the club," John said. "Come on, get dressed. Did you drive here?"

"Yes."

"Good. After we eat, we can restock the larder. It's a lot easier with a car."

"What happened to yours?"

"Up on blocks in a friend's barn. Wasn't worth the cost of running it here."

"How do you manage?"

"Connections. Let's go, Kev, we need some exercise. *Vertical* exercise," he amended, aborting Kevin's smartass response.

Although clouds threatened off the horizon, for the moment the air was bright and clear. There were people about, walking and driving, but not the tourist crowds Kevin had expected. He kept pace as John headed purposefully down the lane. "Connections?"

"Mrs. Herbert, she lives just over there." He nodded toward a narrow terraced house with a bright show of chrysanthemums beneath its front window. "She was a Wren in World War II. Retired now, of course—she's nearly ninety. Can't drive her old Mini anymore, so I take her shopping every week or so."

"From the look of your cupboard, the old girl must be down to her last digestive biscuit. Do we need to stop in and pick up her shopping list?"

"No, she's in London with her family this week. Her granddaughter came down on the train and drove her back. I was just waiting for a dry day to take my bike to Tesco's."

"You have a motorcycle?"

John laughed. "Just two pedals and panniers. It's part of my new routine. When I was in the Balkans, I got to the point where I couldn't function. Completely dissociated, just sat around like a lump, not responding to orders, not doing my job. Even after the active hostilities ended, some of us stayed on—well, you know that. We still have troops over there with the NATO forces."

Kevin nodded.

"I was lucky. My CO knew I wasn't putting it on. They sent me off to a medical unit for observation. What would you rather have, Kev, a real breakfast or something more substantial?"

"I'd like eggs—a fried breakfast, if you know a good restaurant." Kevin didn't react to the abrupt change of subject. He knew John had tried to kill himself when he was under observation, but he was speaking about it in a perfectly normal tone, and Kevin wasn't absolutely sure he wanted to know the details.

"I know just the place, if you don't mind feeling like you're eating in your auntie's cottage."

"If Auntie can cook, I'm all for it."

"When I got to the base hospital, I was really in trouble," John said, as though there'd been no verbal detour. "They made sure I wasn't on drugs—I told them I wasn't using anything, but they didn't want to believe me, so they ran a bunch of tests. I was in officers' quarters then, going in twice a week to talk to a therapist, but the rest of the time all I could do was sit around feeling guilty."

"Guilty? Hell, Johnny, didn't one of the officers in the NATO command blow his brains out over that mess? A colonel, I think."

"Yeah, but that didn't seem to matter. Everyone else in hospital at least had something physical wrong with them. It was the usual sort of self-doubt—sissy boy, cut finger, too weak to pull my weight. They'd already diagnosed me as PTSD, but I just—" He shook his head. "My brain was offline. They'd given me sleeping pills. When the doctor asked if I was feeling suicidal, I said no. I didn't realize what a temptation that whole bottle would be. I can't believe I was so bloody stupid, but at the time it seemed reasonable. I just wanted to stop hurting."

Kevin bit his lip so hard he thought it would bleed. But he didn't think Johnny wanted any response, and he certainly didn't need recriminations.

John shrugged. "Apparently I wasn't quite ready to quit. I passed out, then woke up and wandered out into the car park in my pajamas and collapsed again. Someone found me."

"Thank God."

"After I got out of hospital, got back home, I had to learn that it's a balancing act. I had to start looking after myself instead of going to the base medic. Eventually I found out that for me—it doesn't work for everybody—but for me, getting enough exercise keeps away depression and anxiety. Changes the metabolism. You know I've never been one for pills—now I don't need 'em."

He wasn't sure what to say, but John seemed to be waiting. "That makes sense."

"So when I moved out here to go back to school, I put the car in storage and bought a used bike. Mostly I walk. I manage pretty well, actually. Living on a disability pension's been interesting, learning what I really need. It's less than I'd expected. I'm busy enough with classes that I wouldn't have time to waste even if I did have the money. But the big food shops are outside town, so that takes a little more planning."

"I think an expedition's in order, then," Kevin said. "I left my car in a park down near the Quay."

"Should be safe enough there. I like this season. The weather's sloppy, but it's quiet. Not like summer. Nothing doing until the big Christmas rush."

They turned a corner and there, suddenly, was the sea. Kevin had grown used to being away from it, but there was always that tug, that feeling of coming home, in the wind that blew down the Channel. A few square-riggers, floating museums, sat placidly in their berths, dwarfed in comparison to the modern steel-hulled ships. He wondered how much the old place had really changed since men first sailed out in those wooden vessels, out of reach of their homes, all the lives under their command depending on their captain's skill and good judgment... and his luck. And of the luck to be had, there was always more bad than good, disaster's always waiting for that one mistake....

"Kev? I said it's just down this way, near the Sally Port."

He blinked at John's voice so near his ear, and brought himself back to the present. "Yes. Fine." A few more steps, and his own story started to spill out. "We had an assignment," he said. "Guard four prisoners, suspected terrorists, until someone turned up to transport them. It shouldn't have been any big deal, except that we were originally supposed to release them to military personnel.

"The people who came for them weren't real soldiers—they were some kind of damned no-name mercenaries, the sort of bully-boys who were probably rejects from the real Army. They had the verbal codes, but that was all—and that wasn't enough. I contacted my CO, and he said absolutely not, wait for further orders. So we told the mercenaries to tell their people to call our people. They left—and they came back shooting. That convinced us that they were not legitimate, so we returned fire. I was hit, two of my men were killed."

John touched him on the shoulder, very lightly, as though making sure he was still there. "Was that when you got this?"

"Yeah. And they got our prisoners. Shot one, right there. Another was found a few days later, tortured to death. The other two just disappeared."

"But what else happened, Kev? From what I've heard, that whole area is out of control. Why did they go after you?"

"Everything went wrong all at once," Kevin said. "After the medics got there, and my CO, we had a visitor—another damned mercenary, but a real officer type. I don't know who he was, but he was important. And it turned out—or they decided to put out the story—that there'd been a communication problem. The mercenaries were supposedly sent by someone who had the authority to take custody. My guess is it was someone who wanted those prisoners killed but didn't want official responsibility. There's a lot of that going on."

"But—all right, I see how that would be a problem, but—"

"No, you don't see all of it," Kevin said. "That didn't develop until later. The real problem was the reason they wanted it kept quiet in the first place. One of the prisoners, the one who was killed on the spot, was the son of one of the local officials—very important people in the area. And the family had already come out to the site. They got hold of the body, so there was no way it could be shuffled out of sight. Even worse, some of the family are British citizens. The prisoner's sister is married to a professor of Middle East studies at a university here, and since her brother had been in our custody, they took it to court—sued the Army for failing to protect him. By the time the mess hit the news, the mercenary black-ops team had somehow vanished from the records, so it looked as though my team was either incompetent or criminal."

He stopped again, looking at all the vessels resting so peacefully at anchor in the harbor. The appearance meant nothing. Any one of them could have terrorists aboard. Any of them could hold an intelligence team with long-range sound pickups, monitoring every word he was saying right now. And if so—well, let them listen and be damned. He was saying nothing that had not come out in the inquiry; John's ignorance was an incredible fluke. "Unfortunately, someone, somewhere, decided that the best way to deal with the situation was to let the Army take all the blame. Specifically, to let one officer take the blame and resign."

"*What?*" Johnny looked as though he couldn't believe what he'd just heard. Kevin didn't blame him; that had been his own reaction.

"The mercenaries, whoever they were—and we can both make a good guess where they came from—were sent by someone with friends in high places."

"But why were you—"

"I was the officer in charge."

"But you lost two of your men—and you were shot—how did they explain that?"

"I was allowed to say we had been attacked by unknown forces. And in retrospect, I had made mistakes. Until I was satisfied as to the identity of those mercenaries, I should have disarmed them and locked them up while we waited for better identification. In a hundred other situations, it would have been the sort of mistake I could have learned from. I *did* learn from it, actually, and if I had it to do again, I'd do some things differently, but that's beside the point now."

John let out a huge sigh. "Still… you survived."

"Yes." He met those deep brown eyes, saw no accusation. "Yes, I did."

They started down Broad Street, toward the Sally Port where the old Navy had once launched its boats, back when the deep-bottomed tall ships had to anchor far out in the harbor. The town had changed a lot since the last time Kevin had seen it—new brickwork, new posh row houses, and the Spinnaker building towering over the shore. He hadn't decided yet whether he liked the thing; it was a little too modern for his taste and was yet another piece of the new century obscuring the past. But some things didn't change: the squeaking cries of seabirds still pierced the background hum of engines and pedestrian traffic.

At last John said, "If you hadn't taken responsibility, your team would have been held responsible, wouldn't they?"

"Very likely. And if it *had* been terrorists come to rescue their own, instead of those fucking invisible black-ops, I'd be wearing a medal."

"And instead, you're the scapegoat. If they had any sense—"

"'If' is a handful of dust, Johnny. The bottom line is, *if* the damned fool who thought we were too stupid to tell the difference between military uniforms and fancy-dress toy soldier suits had just sent the mercs in regular uniforms with forged insignia, we'd have released the prisoners without a second thought. If they'd waited fifteen minutes to have their chief send an all clear, none of it would have had to happen. But as far as taking the blame—there was an undeniable murder that happened on my watch. If I hadn't agreed to the story they gave me, we might have been framed for murder. My whole team. I had less to lose—"

"You lost your career!"

The honest anger in John's voice, outrage on his behalf instead of directed against him, was so unexpected it brought tears to his eyes and somehow stiffened his spine as well. There really was someone on his side; he'd forgotten Johnny's fierce loyalty. "Yes, but—honestly, I made a serious mistake, and people died because of it. Granted, my decision was made with insufficient information—there was crucial data that I should have been given—but things could have been much worse. What I admitted to, what I really was guilty of, was nothing more than an error in judgment, and that's not a criminal offense." He shook his head. "It's possible I just wasn't cut out for the work, John. I look at the mistakes I made, and I still don't believe they were necessarily mistakes. A lot of what went wrong on that mission was sheer bad luck."

"Beyond that, I would say." John's voice was neutral. "Beyond even our own Army, it sounds like. I would say criminal conduct on the part of persons unknown."

"Yes. But still, I should have been able to do something."

"Mm." They walked on a little way, and then John said quietly, "You can have some of the guilt, Kev. But—did you ever actually disobey an order? Do anything that you should not have done?"

"What?"

"Or were you behaving in as sane a way as possible, under insane circumstances? Suppose you had decided to disarm the mercs—would they have let you do it?"

"God knows. The bastards might have started a firefight at that point," Kevin admitted.

"So—" John said. "Chain of command, military protocol, you did everything possible. But you were facing an enemy that should have been an ally. You were betrayed. You can't take the blame for that."

For one idiot moment, Kevin was about to argue that yes, he could. "I did."

"Of course you did, love. I can't imagine you doing anything else. Well, here's the place. Do you still feel like eating?"

"Yes!" Surprisingly, that cold lump that he'd been carrying in his gut for the past six weeks—a presence that felt like hunger but never welcomed food—was now gone. He caught the door and held it open, smiling. "You're good, Johnny."

"What?" John's eyebrows went up as a motherly-looking woman walked over to greet them.

"Nothing." Kevin looked around. "You weren't joking—this really *is* Auntie's tea shop, isn't it?" With its chintz curtains, old-fashioned little tables, and antique teapots sitting high on narrow shelves, it looked like the sort of place his grandparents might have visited.

"Yes. But Auntie can cook, and I don't believe this place even has a microwave in the kitchen."

Kevin felt slightly silly doing it, but habit compelled him to sit so he could watch the door, to "accidentally" drop his menu to the floor, and to check the underside of the table for electronics… and to survey the harmless tea shop for potential surprises. He had no reason to expect trouble, but the habit was not likely to extinguish itself easily, and given the uncertain times, he wasn't sure he wanted it to.

"Will it bother you if I order sausages?" Johnny asked in an undertone.

"No, not at all. I'll have some myself. Sausages don't look like meat, really. As long as I don't know what's in it."

"Best not to know, they always say. But you have to be careful taking an unfamiliar sausage from a stranger."

He met John's eyes and saw sheer mischief, felt his own Irish complexion heat up. "God, I can't take you anywhere!"

"I brought you here!" Johnny said innocently.

"Same difference!" He turned his deliberate attention to the menu and managed to maintain his composure while the waitress brought tea and took their orders.

Once that was taken care of, John glanced around and asked quietly, "So what will you do now, Kev? What *can* you do?"

He found it hard to answer, remembering the Colonel hovering around like a vulture, hinting that a resignation would appease the jackals, hinting that a man who came through for his regiment would be "looked after." For some reason he had found that so disgusting that he'd nearly told him to take his offers and stuff them. But he'd held his temper; he could always walk away later, after he'd had time to cool down, think it over, and decide what he really wanted.

"It's not the problem you might think. *Now* I'm the fair-haired boy, with friends in high places. I've been offered a retainer as a 'security advisor,' which means—if I take it—I might be sent off now and then to do something I couldn't discuss. I've been offered a book contract for fiction about our heroic SAS forces—even offered a ghostwriter if I don't think I can express myself in plain English. I think that offer's coming out of a propaganda budget somewhere—at the moment it would be good PR to raise sympathy amongst the general public. There've been hints I could even be offered a job in something less front-office...."

"MI5?"

Kevin wondered what the official policy was on gay partners as security risks. Something less than a wife, no doubt, and he was making a huge assumption about their future together, an assumption he had no right to make. He gave John a wry smile. "Couldn't say. And probably couldn't even if I took the job, which is why I'm not particularly interested. But it seems I never did a better day's work than standing up in that damned court and falling on my sword. Pity all these helpful *friends* couldn't have got me word of those mercenaries just a few minutes sooner."

"Writing fiction would take you right out of the loop."

"Yes, and that's the most attractive aspect of it. If I can't really be *in* the game, I might be better off completely out of it. It's a bit of a stretch, but I might be able to go into security system design, translation, even law enforcement. The big decision, really, is whether to stay involved with the military or make a clean break, walk away."

John nodded. "That's where I've been these past few years too. Trying to decide, retooling my skills. I couldn't stay in military ops, even at a desk. With the way the world is going, I'm told there'll be a need for postcombat counselors. The question is whether I can stand it, even at that remove."

Something tickled at the back of Kevin's mind, but he could not pin it down. "If you can, you'll be one of the best." John looked down, shrugging. "I'm serious. What's the one thing you always hear from men who come back from psych debriefing? 'They weren't there, they don't understand.' You were there, Johnny. Your presence as a counselor would show that there *is* something beyond the crisis—something they can reach for."

"Mm." For a moment John's eyes were focused a long way off, and then he was fully present again. "It's better now, but I'm still not certain. Is there any one of your options that feels more attractive than another?"

"Not really. Not yet. I decided to take a month's holiday and just clear it all out. There is one other possibility: I might teach an academic subject at the training academy. I spent a year as an instructor before they put me in the field, and did pretty well at it."

"Language? Or engineering?"

"Language, probably. Arabic's a high-demand subject now, especially for teachers whose first language is English. I could even apply to civilian colleges. Wouldn't need to keep up on the 'specialty' subjects for that."

"You would be a good teacher."

"I hope so."

"If you stayed with the military, you might stop someone making exactly the same mistakes you did. Or at least warn them about the sort of situation that won't come up in their official briefings."

"That would be something." He took a sip of his tea, finally cool enough to drink. "The single most frustrating—Johnny, when you've had enough of my running whinge, tell me to shut up, will you?"

John just smiled.

"The single worst thing is that there *are* mad, dangerous people out there—yes, some of it's been blown up—" He grimaced, hearing what he'd just said. "Wrong choice of words. Some of it's been… exaggerated by the media. But the danger's still there, and it's worse, much worse than I ever imagined. One assignment we had gave me nightmares—but we contained it, we kept the country safe. And now I'm out of the game."

"It meant a lot to you," John said. "Still does."

"Yeah."

"I don't know what to say…."

"You don't have to. You're listening. That helps." He sighed. "Going by my track record, I can hardly say it will all fall apart if I'm not involved. The game's been played for centuries."

"Millennia. As long as countries have existed and fought one another."

"And I've lost my chance to make a difference."

"Maybe you've already made a difference, love. Maybe you've done your bit, and now you can have a normal life outside the team. You don't have to carry it for the rest of your life."

"I wouldn't have wanted to. But the decision to put it down...." He was startled by the sudden surge of anger that burst past his carefully constructed resignation. "That should have been *mine.*"

John shrugged. "Or you could have died. I'm glad you didn't."

The waitress brought their food, plates heaped with eggs, potatoes, sausage, fried tomatoes, and toast. That delayed conversation for a time and gave him a chance to mull over what John had said—as well as some things he'd not said. Could he have stayed with his regiment, fought the charges, embarrassed the government even further—and come back to Johnny afterward, acknowledged him as a partner?

Not likely. He hadn't even had the nerve to try. He might never have had the nerve. He probably would have let the job eat him alive and accepted that the task was worth the sacrifice. However ugly and stupid the politics might be, he still had no doubt whatsoever that the job was worth doing. Many of their missions had been tiny moves on a massive chessboard, but one of them had been straight out of a Stephen King horror tale, and they'd made a happy ending of it. He and his team had saved at least a million lives when the Russian mafia tried to bring a dirty bomb into the heart of London. And he had been a part of stopping that. Johnny was right. He *had* made a difference, one he could be proud of. Maybe it really was all right to let it go now, and make a life for himself.

The food, even the sausage, was absolutely delicious.

Chapter Six

FINALLY THE plates were cleared, and they decided on one more pot of tea for the road, to give them time to write a grocery list. John dug a crumpled envelope out of his pocket, some kind of advert that had been in his mailbox when they'd left his flat.

"Right, then," he said, printing BREAD in neat letters at the top of the list. "How long can you stay?"

The seemingly innocent question hung in the air between them. Kevin found himself at an uncharacteristic loss. Not knowing what his reception might be, he had not made any plans. Truth be told, he had been running on instinct, with very little higher function involved. He had been shell-shocked and going to ground.

"I—indefinitely, Johnny. As of yesterday noon, I'm more or less a free agent. How long do you want me?"

John's eyes got very big, and he drew a long, careful breath. "Would it sound too treacly romantic if I said 'forever'?"

Kevin swallowed, picking up his own cup to steady himself. He'd half expected that answer; he'd hoped for it. He didn't know how to respond.

And then John added, prosaically, "But I do have an important exam on Tuesday. Statistics."

Kevin sputtered, and half a mouthful of tea went up his nose. "Sorry!" he said, mopping his face. "That's not romantic at all."

John passed his own napkin across the table. "You'd be surprised. At least you're not running for your life at the idea."

Running *toward* life was what it felt like, but for the moment, he had no words.

"Something to think about, anyway," John said, and moved on to something he probably thought was less fraught with emotion. "Where are you living now, in Hereford?"

"Yes. It's a secure flat, owned by the Army. If I accept the consulting offer, I could stay there...." His throat tightened.

"You don't want to?"

"I—I can't. It feels cowardly, but I can't do it. There's too much gone, Johnny, even walking through the door—" He could feel his heartbeat picking up and tensed against the impulse to get up, get out, forced his body to obey his will, just as he had in the courtroom.

"I know," John said. He shifted his hand slightly so his warm fingers rested over Kevin's cold ones. "It's a piece of your life that isn't yours anymore. I felt that way when they gave me a desk job, after I got out of hospital."

"I didn't even go back," Kevin admitted. "I meant to spend yesterday boxing my things, then go find a new flat. But I couldn't go back. Got in the car and started driving. Halfway here I realized I'd better not just show up on your doorstep, I might not be welcome."

"You knew where I was?"

The redirection startled him out of his funk. "Yes. I always have. Just didn't have the nerve to call. I'm sorry."

"The phone works both ways." John gave his hand a quick squeeze. "Let's go. We can finish the list in the car."

Kevin nodded, and by the time they were back on the street, he felt more at ease, even in the light drizzle that had begun while they were inside.

"So you're going to stay for a bit," John said.

"I'd like that, yes. And I can tutor you for that exam."

John blinked. "You could, couldn't you? I forgot how handy you are outside of bed!"

"Oh, thanks!"

"Anytime. But as to food—I'll just figure on provisions for a week and double the quantity. Any special requests?"

"You're out of tea."

"I know."

"What's in that jar in your fridge? Some kind of biology experiment?"

John made a face. "Mrs. Herbert's marmalade. It's horrible. Her memory's wonky—I think she forgot to add sugar, but she always asks if I still have it, and I'm afraid she'll make more if I say it's gone. I think next time I'll ask her to show me how it's done, so I can make sure she gets it right. You didn't actually *eat* any of it—?"

"No. Just curious. I wouldn't mind strawberry jam, then. And, Johnny—you've paid the rent, let me get the groceries, all right?" He'd always been a little better heeled than John, though when they'd been together before, living on identical salaries, it had never been an issue. Now, if Johnny was scraping by on a pension, Kevin was pleased that his money would come in useful. "Anyway, I had a lot of unused leave due, and since I resigned instead of waiting to be thrown out, they paid me for it. And there's the deposit I'll get back from my flat—"

"You'll need that for a new one, though." John pointed to a cross street. "Is it the car park up that way?" Kevin nodded. "I'm not joking, Kev. If you want to stay with me, you're welcome for as long as you like. The place might be small for both of us, though—" He laughed. "Sorry. I don't want to push. I sound like one of Pat's jokes."

"Pat?"

"Massage lady. Do you know what a lesbian drives on the second date?"

"Can't say I've ever dated one. What would she drive?"

"A rent-a-van."

Kevin didn't catch the joke at first, then chuckled. "This is hardly our first date, Johnny. I doubt if there's anyone in the world who knows me better than you do. But we have some catching up to do."

"And a lot of decisions to make. You, especially. But the funny thing is, from the minute I opened the door yesterday, every time I think about the future, it's got you in it—as though whatever the future holds, we'll face it together."

His words had an almost physical resonance. "That's how I feel, too," Kevin said slowly. "I don't think I've ever felt so certain about anything. It's strange. Part of me is saying, yes, go on, this is right, but I don't want to—" He shook his head. Given a task, he could simply focus on it and decide on tactics. This situation, where his real goal was unclear, was as difficult as anything he'd dealt with in the SAS. "I don't want to say yes to you, and find out in six months that it was just some sort of reaction."

"Reaction? To being cast adrift, you mean?"

"I suppose so. The unit was full of conflict, but it was a unit. A kind of belligerent, dysfunctional family. I don't want to use you as a lifeboat and risk hurting you later."

"Mm." They walked in silence for a few steps. Finally John said, "Kev, I've seen your reactions. Unless you've changed a lot, your instincts are usually good. You may not know exactly *why* you choose one thing over another, but it's generally the right choice. Yes, this last one, too," he continued quickly before Kevin could contradict him. "Based on what information you had, you made the best decision you could. The communication problems—hell, the politics—that was all outside your control."

Kevin shook his head. "That's not the point. I can handle the mistakes I made there. I'm not happy with the results, but it was the job, and we all knew the risks. The risks with you...."

"Are half mine." John turned and met his eyes. "My God, Kevin—I lost you once. Do you think I don't understand the risk? I do, perfectly well—and it's my choice. You're worth the risk to me. Worth any risk."

Kevin had to look away at that. He hadn't expected such a naked declaration, such total trust. He didn't feel worthy of it.

Johnny didn't seem to expect a response. "You only have to take responsibility for your half," he said. "Fair enough?"

"Fair enough." Kevin ran a hand through his hair and was surprised at how much water flew off. "Keep reminding me, Johnny. I probably need to hear it."

"Speaking of family, though, what did the Brigadier have to say about all this?"

He could have wished John hadn't brought that up, but now was probably as good a time as any. "Enough. When he got through swearing, he agreed that my resignation was probably the only thing that might save the situation. And after congratulating me on having the balls to face it, he asked me how the hell any son of his could have made such a mistake, and why did I have to ruin myself in public where it would cause him maximum embarrassment."

"Ouch."

"It went better than I'd expected, actually. At least he didn't give me a loaded pistol and leave me to take the gentleman's way out. And in a way, I honestly wonder if he wasn't pleased. *He* never made it into the SAS, you know. He applied—and failed the screening. That was part of why I went out for it. A stupid reason, I know that now. But it was one of the few things he *hadn't* done better than I ever could."

"And you did pass."

"For all the good it did me. I got farther than he did, but his failure wasn't so public. Anyway, I reminded him the family honor wasn't resting solely on my shoulders—he still has Edward and Marian. She married Mark two years back, and they've just produced the first grandson, so his military dynasty is secure. The Brigadier has already started a trust fund for the kid's tuition at Sandhurst. Poor little sod."

"How did your brother and sister react to the mess? And your mum?"

"Ned was embarrassed, said he was sorry I'd had such bad luck—but he reckons the public has a memory shorter than the interval between elections, and he's glad I'm out of the war zone. Marian and my mother want to resurrect Nelson so he can tackle the colonials and do it right this time." He had to smile at the memory of the distaff Kendrick opinion on England's allies and what passed for their intelligence service. "I think there is currently a family boycott on imported goods. And by the way, my mother did ask whether I ever saw that nice Lieutenant Hanson anymore, and said I should feel free to bring you by for dinner if I did. I think she guessed about us, Johnny. Probably the way I kept looking at your bum that time she met us for lunch in London."

"And your father?"

He sighed. "I spoke to him a week before I gave my testimony. I haven't heard from him since, and I don't give a damn what he thinks. I'm sure my mother hasn't said anything to him about you, and neither have I. It isn't worth the energy."

"Do you think you ever will?"

"I suppose so, if it's important to you." He knew he had to say it, but he hoped mightily that John wouldn't ask that of him.

John shrugged. "Not especially. He may be your father, but as far as I'm concerned, it's none of his business. He'll probably figure it out sooner or later, and we can deal with it if and when."

Kevin shook his head. "If he knew, it would only confirm all his worst fears, give him an easy explanation for my failure—he'd say you can't expect a queer to be an effective officer. He'd probably claim my mother got me off the mailman, never mind I look so much like him it's pitiful. That's one thing I suppose really is for the best."

"What's that?"

"The reality check. There I was, in the worst moment of my life, and all he could think about was how my disaster lost face for *him*. Nearly thirty years, and I finally saw the situation clearly. I spent my whole damned life trying to make him proud of me, and now that I know it's impossible, it's actually a relief! No more jumping at a hurdle that moves every time I try. I'm going to live the rest of my life so I'm satisfied with it myself, and if it's not good enough for him, too damned bad."

"You didn't fail, Kev. You made a decision and caught the world's worst luck."

"I was in command. And I did fail. But it isn't the end of the world."

"You survived it. So did most of your men."

"You said that before."

"Because it's important," Johnny said. "If I had to go into the field under your command or your father's—who do you think I'd pick?"

"That's not a fair question. You can't stand my father."

"There is that." John grinned. "I hope to be 'serving under you' as soon as we get home, and I wouldn't spend time in the same room as your father if I could avoid it. But seriously, love, do you know anyone who hasn't failed at something, or at least made huge mistakes?"

"That wasn't what I meant."

"I'm sorry—I'm not trying to put words in your mouth. But what you're saying reminds me of how I felt when things started falling apart, and I needed help to figure it out afterward. When every decision can mean life or death, the responsibility becomes intense. It's a burden, but it gives you a little sense of security, too. You tell yourself that if you do everything just right, your team will be safe. It's an illusion, of course—no one can do everything just right, and even if you did, the enemy has a nasty habit of changing the program. And you feel the weight either way." He laughed suddenly. "Sorry. This is basic stuff about control issues. If I have to remind you not to be too responsible, you should remind me not to lecture."

"I will, but only when you stop making sense." Why had no one ever mentioned that in training? Had they been banking on his sense of responsibility, his expendability? But he had no cause for complaint, or even surprise. *Why* someone did something mattered only insofar as it was a way of eliciting performance. Individuals in the Army were supposed to be interchangeable—interchangeable, and, when necessary, expendable. That was how the system worked.

And he felt, for the first time, a deep sense of relief that he was no longer an interchangeable, disposable part of that system.

"The car's over there. The little blue job."

The drive to Sainsbury's and the shopping expedition itself were uneventful. Kevin made a point of replacing the beer they'd wiped out the night before, and steered toward the deli section for what amounted to a picnic lunch. John protested at first, but saw the sense in Kevin's argument that it would be better to spend the rest of the day in bed than in the kitchen. The staple items—milk, eggs, bread, and the like—were supplemented by a few more exotic ingredients that Kevin had plans for. All in all, the trip was a peaceful, successful reprovisioning foray.

It was on the drive home that things began to get complicated.

Kevin had just negotiated a tricky turn, complicated by the presence of a white van whose driver had apparently won his license in a lottery. He'd gotten the car straightened out on the wet road when Johnny shouted, "Stop!"

Chapter Seven

COMBAT REFLEXES made for interesting driving. The car skidded and fought him as he braked and steered onto the shoulder. The van's taillights were disappearing in the distance, and there was no one else on the road, which helped.

He asked, "What is it?" but John was already out of the car and sprinting back down the road. Lovely. He set the emergency blinkers going and followed, hoping Johnny hadn't spotted a corpse or something equally awful.

"Poor little bastard," John said when he got close.

"What? Is someone hurt—oh Christ."

It wasn't a body—or, rather, it was a body, but not a human one. A brown-splotched cat had apparently tried to cross but had been no match for tons of motorized steel. Which was a pity, but hardly worth stopping for—except for the kitten huddled against its mother's body, standing on wobbly legs and squalling its indignation to the world.

"We can't just abandon it," John said.

"I suppose not, but what will you do with it?"

"I don't know, but I'm not going to leave it to be squashed. Watch for traffic, would you? I don't want to frighten him into the road." John got down on all fours, dignity forgotten, and crept toward the little beast, who was either too frightened, too overwhelmed, or too bloody-minded to flee from the big hands that encircled him. "Got you! Oh, damn!"

Monitoring the road, Kevin glanced down briefly. "What?"

"There's two of them. Mother's dead for certain. Cold. Come on, love… that's right, I'm only here to help…." He stood up with his prizes—two damp kittens. The screamer was marmalade with a white apron, the timid one a little black-and-white job.

Kevin accepted the second, holding the soggy infant against his body to keep it warm. "Now what?"

"We'd better look around, I think. Two kittens isn't a very big litter."

"Big enough," Kevin said, but he made no objection to searching the roadside. By the time they'd covered half a mile or so, though, the rain had picked up and there was no sign of life. "Johnny, if she's raised 'em feral, these may be all that survived. Foxes, owls, dogs…. That might've been why she was moving them."

"I suppose you're right." He looked around one last time. "Let's get these little orphans out of the storm. Do you think they're weaned?"

"God, I hope so!" He handed the second kitten over to John so he could concentrate on getting them back home in one piece. "Now what?"

"Well, they've got teeth. I suppose that means they've started eating solid food. Um, dry 'em off, get some warm food into 'em. Would you mind very much going back to Sainsbury's?"

"I'd just as soon keep on. Is there any place in Portsmouth we can find cat food?"

"I'm sure there is." John unzipped his jacket halfway and tucked both kittens inside, next to his body. "In fact, I can phone Pat and see if she's got any suggestions. She can probably loan us a few tins. I don't suppose they'll eat much."

"She doesn't have a nice motherly cat, does she?"

"Unfortunately, no. They've got four already, all fixed. Oh, shite!"

"What?"

"We'll need a litter pan as well. And I'll have to wash this shirt."

Kevin was finding it difficult to keep a straight face. "John. Are you planning to keep these animals?"

"I couldn't just leave them out there, could I? And who knows what will happen if I turn them over to…. Yes, I'd like to. Unless you're allergic, or hate cats. You don't, do you?"

Kevin glanced over. The yellow kitten was halfway out of the jacket, gnawing on Johnny's finger. There was nothing visible of the other but a pair of huge frightened eyes above a pink nose. And John himself was clearly smitten. "No, I don't. My mother's always had a few moggies around. I don't mind."

Kevin had a strange premonition of domesticity: the two of them as old codgers, tottering around a cottage in the Cotswolds, surrounded by a petting zoo. Amazingly, the image wasn't as awful as he would have thought. In a way it was a treat to be concerning himself with the fate of two small felines instead of a gang of hot-tempered, quarrelsome, heavily armed humans and the safety of all of Britain. "Most animals are more reasonable than most humans, come to that. Though I don't fancy increasing the family beyond these two, and I'm not looking forward to them screeching us awake at five in the morning."

"That's parrots. Cats just climb all over you."

"Lovely. Well, they can't weigh much. But just these two, Johnny. And no goats."

"I'm the one who'll wake you up climbing on you," John promised. "You'll never notice the cats. No goats, no chickens, no cows and sheep, unless you decide you want to try your hand at farming."

"I'll hold you to that."

"No lions, no tigers…." He wasn't really talking to Kevin. The little cat had all four legs wrapped around his hand, acting as though he was about to bring this big catch down any minute.

"What're you going to call them?"

"Best to find out if they're Tom or Thomasina first, don't you think?" John pulled his hand a few inches away and the kitten flung himself onto it.

"That's a lad," Kevin said with conviction. "Rugby player. The other one's his baby sister."

"I think you're right." He captured the young predator and held it up to his face. "Pay attention, sir. What would you say to Horatio?"

Kevin hooted. "Horatio?"

"Well, it is Portsmouth, and he's got yellow hair. Fur."

"Nelson? Dear God."

"Don't know. Maybe the old Roman at the bridge. If he hadn't been standing there, I'd never have seen either of them. He's Nelson right now, undersized and feisty. But he might grow up to be an Admiral—"

"Johnny, it's a cat!"

"Then the last name doesn't matter. He can have one of ours."

"What about the other one?"

"I don't know yet. She's asleep."

"Still—Horatio?"

"I've been working on a project for one of my classes. We have to do a psych profile of a historical figure, come up with a plausible diagnosis, identify the dysfunction or disorder, speculate on causes, or take a disorder and find someone who fits the diagnosis, then do a workup of that. You know—Bonaparte had a Napoleonic complex, that sort of thing, only seriously."

"You're psychoanalyzing *Nelson*?"

"Well, not psychoanalysis, exactly, but why not? He was an interesting case. Look at him: humble upbringing, physically small, massive ambition—he might have been overcompensating, but he had the ability to pull it off. Massive ego, too, but where Bonaparte was all about himself, Nelson really was dedicated to his country. He had a brilliant career up to a point, but then he got involved with Hamilton's wife, contrary to any kind of good sense, and that was a financial and political disaster for him. What I suspect is that he may have been suffering from brain damage. Until the injury that reduced his eyesight, he appeared to be a devoted husband, attentive and affectionate. After he recovered, he insulted his wife in public and ran around with Emma. Brain injuries can cause that sort of change in behavior and personality."

Kevin found himself unwillingly interested, carried along by John's enthusiasm. "But nothing else was affected, was it? He was just as effective an officer."

"Yes, that's part of what's so interesting. You'd expect more dysfunction, but if anything he just got better at what he did. He even took advantage of the disability—that old story about disregarding orders by holding his telescope to his blind eye so he couldn't see the signal flags. Of course, by then his men loved him so much that he could do no wrong in their eyes."

"I suppose you're in the right place for the research, too."

John laughed. "Absolutely. You'd be surprised at how much grief I've been given for criticizing the man. But I never meant it that way. What he was able to accomplish, as small as he was and missing an eye as well as an arm—having only one eye meant no depth perception—he was really phenomenal. Especially when you think about what life was like then, with men stuck on those tiny ships for months or years at a time."

"Rum, sodomy, and the lash," Kevin teased. "Kiss me, Hardy! Is there something you're not telling me, Johnny? All the sailors around here…?"

"God, no!" John shook his head. "It's interesting to study, but the system was completely mad. Literally—sailors had ten times the insanity rate of landsmen, and it's hard to say whether it was the horrible living conditions, or the half-pint of rum every day killing off brain cells, or the surgeons pumping the poor bastards full of mercury as a cure for the pox. Amazing that the Navy worked as well as it did. I suppose the French and Spanish were even worse off. But I think I may have found the key—" He laughed. "Sorry, Kev, I expect it's pretty boring if you're not involved."

"You've never bored me. If you're enjoying the class that much, it sounds like you've got the right line of work."

"I think I finally have. I always thought of myself charging off to do battle, but—I suppose someone has to patch up the warriors who come dragging back. It's useful, at least."

Kevin didn't like the self-deprecation. "You're as much a warrior as any of them. There'll be men who walk away whole again because you'll show them it can be done."

John swallowed hard and let go of the kitten long enough to rest a hand on Kevin's thigh. "Do you know what it means to have you believe in me like this?"

He took his eyes from the road long enough to meet John's for an instant. "Yes. Exactly." He smiled as he returned his attention to driving. "Don't you realize you're doing the same for me?"

"Oh...." John yelped as young Horatio climbed up his chest. "Damn, he's sharp! Kev, would you mind meeting a friend of mine? I'd like her to take a look at these two."

"Is this your massage guru?"

"Don't let her hear you say that—but yes. I think she'd know how to trim his claws. They're so tiny I don't want to risk it."

"After that treatment you gave me, I suppose I owe her my thanks," Kevin said. "The mobile phone's in my jacket pocket. Can I drop you off and go pick up the cat necessities?"

"You can, but I'd really like you to meet her. And I'd like for her to meet you, too. I'm afraid I've talked about you a lot, and it would be nice to prove that you aren't just a figment of my imagination."

Kevin mulled that over while Johnny found the phone and made the call. He was surprised to find he was harboring a speck of envy toward this unknown woman who had come to assume a place of importance in Johnny's life. There was obviously no reason for the feeling, and he'd been gone so long he was damned lucky John hadn't settled down with some other man. Still....

His anxiety was dispelled when the door of a narrow house swung open to reveal a middle-sized, middle-aged woman with wire-rimmed bifocals, hair trimmed to a neat dark cap liberally mixed with gray—hardly the image of a seductive siren. "John! Come in, I put the kettle on when you called. Where are the babies?"

"Right here, the filthy beasts. Pat, I want you to meet Kevin. I've told you about him. He just got into town last night. Kevin, this is Pat Sullivan-Chalton."

"Good lord, you're real!" She took Kevin's hand, and her sharp green eyes gave him the impression that he was being sized up by an expert. "I'm very glad to meet you. Come in, please. Tess is at work, she had to go teach one of her clients how to use his new website. Would you like something to eat, or some tea?"

"Just tea, thanks," John said. "We had a big late breakfast."

She glanced at Kevin and grinned. "The very best kind."

Johnny actually blushed. "I just need some advice, Pat—and if you have an old shirt of some kind I might borrow—it wasn't just the rain."

She laughed as he opened his jacket. "Jumping right into fatherhood, aren't you? Well, babies of any species are messy. Have a seat. I'm sure I can find something."

After pouring out three cups of tea, she left them sitting at the kitchen table and disappeared down a short hall. To John's questioning look, Kevin said, "She reminds me of my mum."

"She's been a big help—and a good friend. Oh, there's something else—"

"Here you go." Pat had returned, followed by a huge fluffy tiger cat who strolled up and sniffed each man's trouser legs. Kevin extended a few fingers for him to inspect and was rewarded with a vigorous head-butt.

"Congratulations. Shadow approves." Pat held out a dark green sweatshirt. "I think this will fit well enough for now. Would you like to clean yourself up?"

"Yes, thanks." Johnny hung his jacket on the back of the chair and handed one kitten each to her and Kevin. As she exclaimed over the marmalade kitten, John went off down the hall to wash up.

"Thanks for taking the time for this," Kevin said.

"It's no trouble." She smiled warmly. "I've been telling John for ages that he needs a cat to look after him, but he seems to have hit the jackpot all at once. Two cats, and a long-lost—what's brought you into town? Oh, never mind. I saw the news. The pictures of you were terrible, nothing like the one John showed me. I wasn't completely sure it was you, but the name matched. He never mentioned it—I wondered if he'd heard of it at all."

"No, he hadn't." Kevin shifted, uncomfortable. "I told him."

Her keen, inquisitive expression softened. "And he'd have welcomed you just the same if you really had been to blame. He was so certain you were gone forever, and—well, I'd better not say any more. Sorry to pry. It's just that John's such a dear, and I'd love to see him settle down with the right man. They say the one drawback of a happy marriage is that you want to see all your friends in one, too."

"That doesn't sound like a drawback."

An eyebrow lifted. "It's so good to hear you say that. Now, then, what can you tell me about these waifs?"

"Not very much. On our way back from shopping, John saw their mother lying dead by the road—hit by a car, I suppose—then he spotted that little chap. We went back and picked them up—we could only find the two of them. We're not sure if they're boys, girls, or one of each. Oh, and John was hoping you could trim their claws. He's already lost some blood."

"Oh, dear. Well, I'd say this lad is five or six weeks, no older. He has teeth, but you see his eyes? Still that bluish-gray, like human babies. And I do believe he's a lad, though that's hard to tell at this age. He looks old enough for solid food, which will make your lives easier, but they'll need feeding every few hours."

"Like babies?"

"Oh, you can leave dry kibble out for them overnight. And a nail clipper should do the trick for the sharp bits. I can show you or John how to do it. Who will they be living with?"

"Um...."

"*Both* of you? You're back together? How wonderful!"

"Yes, I think so." He blinked. If this woman ever decided to leave massage and go into interrogation, she'd be a natural. "We may need to find a bigger place, but John is so close to finishing his degree, it would be silly to leave Portsmouth now." The words coming out of his mouth surprised him, and so did the feeling of warm anticipation that came with them. This decision, which from the outside must look very spur-of-the-moment, felt unaccountably right. "We haven't worked out any details yet, of course."

"'Where will wants not, a way opens.'" She passed Horatio back to Kevin, took the other kitten, and gently rolled it over. The kitten purred and batted at her fingers. "I'd guess this one's a little girl. Yes, you're a pretty baby, a real tuxedo cat. I love the black stripe on her nose. Do they have names yet?"

"This one's Horatio," he admitted. "We haven't thought of one for her."

"Ah, then you must have heard about John's pet project by now. But this child doesn't look like Emma Hamilton to me, and you'd be daft to breed siblings, anyway."

"Two is plenty!" Kevin interjected.

"That was what I thought, but Tess and I each had two to start, and a fourth always seems to turn up if we lose one." She nodded toward the hall, and he saw that two more cats, a hulking black beast and a tabby, were observing from a safe distance.

"Yes, that's a good kitty," Pat crooned to the kitten. "Having a pair will save you time. They'll keep each other's ears clean and amuse one another. You ought to get them to Simko's vet clinic as soon as you can for a checkup. She's the best in the county. I don't see any fleas, which is a wonder, but the cool weather may have helped on that score. You will need to have them wormed, though."

John came back in time to catch the last comment. "Wormed? Do they really need that?"

"Look at their little bellies! They aren't round like that because they're well-fed. Almost all kittens get intestinal parasites. With strays, it's a certainty—and some of them can infect humans. You really do not want a case of roundworms." Kevin stifled a grin; he knew Pat was no relation of his, but she sounded enough like his mother to be her sister. "It's easy enough to treat them," she continued. "Just two doses of the medicine, two weeks apart. But they absolutely must see a vet. If not today, as soon as you can."

"I thought we could just take them home and get them settled," John said dubiously.

"You're probably right. They don't need any more fuss today. Do you have food? No, John said not. I can give you a couple of tins, but they'll do better on kibble made up specially for kittens...." She frowned. "You'll also need a litter pan. I have a cardboard box that should do for now, and I'll give you litter to start them off."

"How do we know they'll use it?" Kevin asked. "I remember Mum's cat teaching her kittens."

"Well, they're old enough that their mother has probably taught them to bury their messes. For all we know, they may have been indoor pets, abandoned once the novelty wore off—and don't get me started on the bastards who do that! After you feed them, pop 'em into the box and wait until something happens. You can take their front paws and scratch the sand with them, that sometimes gives them a clue."

The mental image was beyond anything he had ever faced in the SAS. "You aren't joking, are you?"

"I'm afraid not. I'd say just leave them with me for a day or two and let Éowyn teach them, but it would be better for you to get them to a vet before you let them socialize with other cats, have them tested for feline leukemia, FIV, all the contagious diseases. Ours have been vaccinated, but that's never a hundred percent certain."

"They look healthy enough," John said.

"They certainly do, and apart from the worms, I expect they are. Here, let me trim their little toes, and you can get them home and fed. Don't give them saucers of cow's milk—they aren't calves. Water is better for them, preferably bottled or filtered water, and not too cold. Let me show you how to tell if they're dehydrated...."

They left a few minutes later, armed with an invitation to dinner sometime soon, more cat-care instructions than they were likely to remember, including the need to buy or build a scratching post, the vet's phone number, a book on cat care, plus the loan of a cat carrier loaded with food, litter, and a pair of dishes outgrown by Pat's menagerie.

Kevin hefted the baggage—John was carrying the kittens, of course—and whistled. "That was quite a briefing. And I think they've got more luggage than I have!"

"There are two of 'em, Kev. And they're just babies."

And Johnny's protective streak was operating at full throttle. "I'm glad I got to you first, or you might not have had room for me!"

"Oh, they're not very big. I think I could've found you a little bed space."

"Then let's get back to it!" He took a breath and let growing certainty override his niggling doubts. "Once we get these little buggers settled, we need to find a bigger place... or at least put my things in storage. I'll have to go back and hire that rent-a-van. Will you come with me and help me clear out my flat in Hereford?"

Johnny turned, open-mouthed, then smiled like sunshine and kissed him, right there in the street. It was only a quick one, but Kevin was relieved there wasn't anyone else around—and then angry at his own reaction. He'd spent a long time undercover—and in the closet. Too long. Damn it, he did love John, he was going to move in with him, and they had every legal right to do so! This might be Portsmouth, but it wasn't the Portsmouth of the bad old days. Their love was no longer a hanging offense. In for a penny, in for a pound, and if that gave the Brigadier fits, so be it.

"I'm sorry," John said quickly, taking his preoccupation for unease.

"Well, I'm not! You just surprised me. But let's go home. I can't do what I'd like to until you put those cats down, and I haven't a free hand to do it with."

He was going to have to make a few phone calls when they got back to Johnny's apartment. The Naval training program in Portsmouth was a potential employer, and he wouldn't need a full-time job while he tried to see if he could be Britain's answer to Tom Clancy.

Chapter Eight

"KEV?"

"Mmm?"

"Will I squash anyone if I move?"

"No, I think they're under the bed. Wait! Can you hear that?"

"What?"

"Someone's in the loo, scratching in the litter box."

"Oh, good. One of the cats?"

"Of course, one of the cats, idiot! Who d'you think?"

"Don't want to think right now. C'mere...."

"What, again?"

"We've only caught up about three months' worth of that seven years' famine."

"Oh. Well, then, roll over. You look like you need your back rubbed...."

"How did you know?"

John rolled over and made himself comfortable, half dozing as Kevin worked his way carefully up one leg, then the other. His touch was a bit tentative but grew more sure as he worked farther up. It wasn't about technique, anyway. Just having him there, making the effort, was sheer heaven. The all-over touching made arousal something more than a reflex, and by the time Kevin entered him, he was floating on an endorphin high. In his admittedly limited experience, there had never been anyone so empathic, so thoughtful; he had never been to bed with anyone who was as much concerned with giving pleasure as getting it. Though there wasn't much doubt that Kevin was enjoying himself too. This wasn't just sex; it was a whole magnitude better, the sort of lovemaking he had remembered with longing but never really expected to find again.

He wasn't sleepy afterward. Kevin went out like a light, though, and John guessed that he had been living under such strain that his body had a sleep debt the size of Kilimanjaro. The thought of actually getting out of bed and finding that statistics text was a little more work than he was prepared to tackle, so he propped a pillow under his head and lay back to watch his lover snore. *If I find his snore romantic, I must be totally besotted.* But it could have been any sound; it wasn't much of a snore, more a reminder that Kevin was here, he was back… and this time it might just be for good.

John could not quite believe his amazing good fortune. Even asleep, with those magical blue eyes shut, Kevin was the most beautiful creature he had ever seen. And it wasn't just physical beauty, though that was indisputable. Kevin had a sweetness about him, a consideration for others, that made him unique. Stopping at Pat's had not been high on Kev's to-do list, but he had gone along willingly enough and had even seemed to have a good time.

Which brought another matter suddenly to John's mind. How was he going to explain—or even describe—his entire relationship with those women? And the impending complications?

It wasn't as though you ever expected to see him again, his mind pointed out. *It's none of his business, really—it's not something you need to bother him about.*

No, of course not. Much simpler to just wait and let him be surprised.

Right.

Young Horatio, tired of pouncing on his sister, came scampering into the bedroom, front legs just barely keeping a jump ahead of the rear, and headed straight for the bed. He caught the dangling edge of a blanket and swarmed up, making a beeline for John's outstretched finger. The hand attached to that finger was bigger than the kitten's entire body, but that made no difference at all in the little fellow's balls-out attack.

"You must be Nelson," John said. "Never mind maneuvers, go straight at 'em."

Horatio ran up to his shoulder, looked around wildly, came to some feather-brained conclusion, and leapt onto Kevin's chest.

The result frightened them all.

With a shout, Kevin threw out his arm, sending Horatio flying across the room. His elbow caught John on the chin. John blinked and went with his instinct, which was to roll over onto his lover and pin him down. As Kevin's eyes opened, John caught a movement out of the corner of his own eye. Horatio had been flung onto the chair beside his chest of drawers and was clinging to the afghan Tess had knitted to cover the chair's ancient, ugly cushions.

The kitten was fine. Kevin was not; he looked stricken. "What did I do?"

"Bounced the cat off the bed. It's all right."

"Johnny, what did I *do*?" He was flushed, breathing hard; his eyes darted around the room.

"That's all, love. You bumped me, so I thought—"

"I could have killed you."

"You didn't."

"But—what happened?"

"Horatio jumped on you—the boy's got good taste—and you knocked him away."

"Did I hurt him?"

Horatio meeped indignantly, gathered himself on the chair, and flung himself at the bed. He missed, but his claws caught halfway down the blanket and he hung there, squalling.

"I don't think so." John leaned over to detach the youngster and held him out for Kevin's inspection. "You may have dented his self-image. I think he was a lion in a former life."

Kevin's smile was forced. He took the kitten carefully and set it down on John's bare stomach. "That's something I didn't mention, though you've probably seen some of it yourself. Postcombat reflexes. I'm not the safest person to share a bed with."

John knew that was a valid fear; he checked his first impulse to say something dismissive. "You weren't sleeping violently, Kev. You reacted to this twit landing on you. Do you wake violently?"

"I don't know. I've had some violent dreams. That last mission—and the training…."

"I'll keep an eye on you, but so far you've just slept quietly. I'd rather not borrow trouble. Have you had violent dreams while you've been here, dreams that woke you?"

"Last night."

"Well, I'm a light sleeper, and whatever you did, it didn't disturb me. The cats might make things more interesting. Or there's something else we can try, if you like. It got the corpses out of my head." At Kevin's frown, he explained. "When I slept—after the Balkans—I kept seeing all the dead civilians from Kosovo, sometimes for hours. Women, kids, animals—I don't go to horror movies anymore, I had my own private screening every night. The dreams got so bad I was afraid to sleep. Pills didn't stop it, and I didn't like the side effects, so I tried hypnosis, and that worked. I've taken some training in hypnotherapy, but if you'd rather do it yourself, I could make a script and you could read it onto a tape."

"I'd rather work with you," Kevin said, settling back onto his pillow. "I've learned a few tricks, counter-interrogation techniques, that sort of thing. Funny it never occurred to me to use it for this. What sort of commands would you use?"

"Suggestions, I'd call them." He gave Kevin's arm a gentle squeeze. "We can start with something simple. Since you're worried about causing harm when you wake up, the best simple suggestion would be to tell your subconscious that when you're sleeping, you should wait until you're completely awake before you react physically. That only costs a fraction of a second. We can work on the language so that it's phrased exactly the way you want."

Kevin looked at him quizzically. "I knew it would be good to see you again. It never crossed my mind that you could do so much."

John shook his head. "You might want to wait and see how much I actually know. I've made recordings for myself, but I've only ever done this for other people in the classroom."

Kevin pulled him over for a kiss. He wasn't able to give the matter his full attention, though, because Horatio climbed up behind him and started chewing on Johnny's long hair.

"What the hell?" Kevin sat up. "When did we last feed those beasts? What time is it, anyway?"

"Nearly midnight. It's been about four hours…. Come to that, when did we last feed *us*?"

"Breakfast." One hand wandered south of John's equator. "That is, if you're referring to actual food."

John knew if he responded to that wicked smile, they'd get nothing to eat before sunrise. "High time for all of us, then. I'll fix something for the kids, you can organize our picnic." He'd gotten two steps toward the door when the little female wrapped herself around his ankle. "Damn it!"

"I don't suppose you can hypnotize cats?"

Johnny had one of them in each hand now, and they were both trying to wriggle free. "Somehow I don't think they'd notice my telling them to relax. Have you come up with a name for her yet?"

"Not really. What's wrong with Emma?"

"She's his sister, Kev!"

"They're *cats*, Johnny! Oh, hell, name her after my mother. Mum would be tickled."

John set the animals down on the kitchen floor. "What—Kate?"

"Kitty! It's very sensible."

"It's not very original."

"Watch." Kevin was at the fridge; he took the tin of cat food, held it out, and called, "Here, Kitty!" The response was immediate—both struggled out of John's grasp and ran to the food. "See? She likes it."

"I suppose. And Kitty will do for now." He warmed some water in the microwave and mixed a little into the chilled cat food, as Pat had instructed, and set out some of the dry kibble on a paper plate. They gobbled the warm food first and immediately proceeded to the other dish. "I'd better call the vet tomorrow. They look like they're going to burst."

"You could call and leave a message now. I'm sure the vet has some kind of voice mail. But they look happy enough to me." Horatio was now standing in the center of the plate, while his sister nibbled daintily from one side. "Go on, Johnny, I've got this in hand."

He really did. In the few minutes it took John to call the vet and leave a message asking for an appointment, Kevin had spread a picnic out across the kitchen counter. "I don't think they can jump this high yet," he explained, nodding toward Kitty, who'd parked herself at his feet. She had abandoned the dry kibble as soon as she'd smelled something more interesting, and was staring upward with a look almost cross-eyed in its intensity.

"They will soon, though," John said. "Chicken is a great motivator."

"Then we'll get a table. And we'll teach them to stay off—at least during meals. My mother used a squirt gun."

The thought of Kevin's poised, elegant mother wielding such a weapon was inconceivable. "Kev… not really?"

"Really. It worked, too. Harmless, but they don't like it." He handed John a plate. "Here, take what you like, and I'll open the champagne."

"Champagne?"

"I thought the occasion deserved it."

Potato salad, chicken salad, half a dozen other containers whose contents he recognized and at least two he didn't, plus a loaf of fresh crusty bread. Kevin had gone a little overboard on the selection; they had enough here for at least one more meal.

"We'll have to drink that from water glasses," John said. "It's that or teacups."

"As long as we don't have to drink from each other's shoes," Kevin said as they settled on the futon. "Here you go, then. To our future together!"

John smiled, but sipped uneasily. There was one more thing he had to tell Kevin, and the sooner he did, the sooner he'd stop feeling guilty. "Kev, it's been a long time since we've seen each other."

"I know. I really should have called you before now, Johnny. I'm sorry."

"It isn't that. That is, in a way—"

"There's someone else?"

"*No!*" He tried to decide how to explain, and realized that no matter what he said, it was going to sound like an outtake from a soap opera. "No, not exactly."

Kevin's expression grew guarded. "That really seems to be an 'either-or' sort of thing, John."

John put his hand over Kevin's. Kev didn't pull away, but he didn't relax either. "No, please listen, it's complicated. I am not interested in anyone else as a lover. I want you. I want *only* you. For the rest of my life, if you'll have me."

"But?" Kevin said warily.

"But...." He hoped this didn't sound as wild to Kevin as it had the first time he'd heard the proposition. "But—you've met Pat."

"Yes," Kevin agreed, clearly at sea. "I have met Pat."

"She and her partner Tess want to have a baby. Two, actually."

"How nice. But.... Isn't she a little old for that?"

"I think she's about forty-five, and I'm not sure if that's really too old, for some women. But Tess is ten or twelve years younger, she's the one actually having them. It. Him or her."

"Oh!" Kevin looked much relieved. "So.... Are you saying you've agreed to be a sperm donor or something? Or—or sleep with her just to, to...."

He hesitated, and John quickly jumped in. "Sperm donor. They'd tried frozen, and it was costing a lot and didn't seem to be working."

Kevin frowned at his plate. "This is really a *lot* more than I wanted to know about those ladies, Johnny." He stabbed at a chunk of potato salad and chewed ferociously.

John couldn't help laughing. Poor Kevin. A classic case of Too Much Information. "I know it must be. And I'm sorry. It's the timing. If they'd just asked recently, I'd tell them I wouldn't do it unless it was all right with you. If I'd ever guessed you might be back, I would have waited—but there wasn't anyone else for me, and it didn't look as if there ever would be, and they wanted me to spend time with the kid, especially if it turned out to be a boy. I was a little worried about the responsibility, but since I don't have any other family, and I think they'll be good mothers.... At any rate," he said, floundering and desperate to get it over with, "I'm going to have a baby. I mean—" Kevin choked, and John pounded him on the back. "I mean, Tess is already pregnant."

"Thank God!"

"What?"

"That it's not you! Well, here's to the new arrival…." He drained the glass. "Just tell me, Johnny—have all the shoes dropped, or is there a half-shod centipede on the roof?"

"I'm sorry, Kev. I really am. It's just that things are moving so fast with us, and a baby's a big thing to keep secret. I don't want to have secrets like that from you. It wouldn't be fair, and I'd feel like some dunce in a soap opera."

"It wouldn't have stayed secret for long! Though I don't think I ever would have had the nerve to ask Pat who the father was."

"I suspect she'd have told you…. After all, you'll be part of the family."

"I will, won't I?" Kevin looked a bit dazed. "What's your obligation, exactly?"

"Legally, none. They had a solicitor draw up paperwork. I'm not legally responsible for anything, though if anything were to happen to both of them, we all agreed that I'd take over, as the natural father. That's also in the agreement. So if you and I are together, there'd be a slight chance you might wind up with a stepson or stepdaughter. Which is why I had to tell you, in case you don't want the responsibility. Not that you'd have to take over, but I might…. Kev, are you all right?"

Kevin had put his fork down on his tray, leaned back, and shut his eyes. "I'm fine. I'm just trying to keep track of everything. You, two cats, a baby on the way, some sort of lesbian in-laws—I don't know what exactly you'd call them, sisters-in-law? Out-laws? And I have to find a new job, and *we* have to find a new home. Have I got it all?"

John thought about it. "I have a test next week. But that's not as important. I'll do well enough in the course even if I blow off the exam." That wasn't entirely true; he'd pass, but barely. Somehow, though, getting good marks didn't seem as important as it had a day or two ago.

Kevin saw it differently. "You can't blow off your exam with a kid on the way." A corner of his mouth quirked upward. "I wonder if it'll look like you? God, my mother will be in seventh heaven when she finds out there'll be another baby in the extended family."

"Your father'll be tearing his hair."

"He can learn to adapt," Kevin said heartlessly. "Do him good."

John sipped at his champagne and studied his lover. Kevin had always been resilient, but this easy acceptance was just astonishing. "No second thoughts?"

Kevin shook his head. "No. Oh, I imagine the first time we have to babysit I'll wonder what on earth I was thinking, but, no, Johnny. When I got here yesterday, I really thought—" He sighed. "I'm not sure what I thought. The future looked pretty empty. Now, I don't know what to expect, but I'm sure it won't be—*whoa!*" He snagged Horatio out of midair, making a leap for his plate. "Dull," he finished, putting the cat back on the floor.

"I see what you meant about a squirt gun," John said.

"Maybe two. Do you have a lease here?"

"I have to give a month's notice. That would put us into a week or two before Christmas."

"So if we found a place we could occupy December first, we'd have a week or two overlap, maybe stay here until the new year. I can put my furniture in storage until then. Unless you're having second thoughts?"

"I feel like a kid on Christmas morning," John admitted. "The only reason I might want to wait would be so we don't rush into something we could regret. I don't think I ever will, but it would be a big change for us both."

"But it's not new," Kevin said. "We've known each other for—how long? Nearly a year, not counting the time we were apart. We've seen each other in a lot of different situations. We know we're compatible."

"You don't have to convince me, love."

"I think I'm convincing myself. I'd always expected to be settled down by the time I was thirty, set in a career, at least thinking about buying a house, getting married, starting a family—then I met you, and kids didn't seem all that important. Then I realized, a little too late, that I couldn't have you and the SAS, and then I made a big mistake." He shrugged. "I'd rather have you."

"I'm sorry you lost your regiment," John said. "But there's something I've been trying to remember. From Tolkien... keep the wee beasts off my plate." He got up and took the third volume from his bookshelf, searching the last few pages as he settled back down beside Kevin. "Here it is. This is exactly what happened to you, love, it's the part where Sam realizes Frodo can't ever go back to how things were before: '…it has been saved,'" he read, "'but not for me. It must often be so, Sam, when things are in danger: some one has to give them up, lose them, so that others may keep them.'" He looked up and saw tears in Kevin's eyes. "You did that for them, gave it up so they could keep it." He put an arm around his lover, hugging him tight. "I hope they appreciated it. The men, I mean, not the brass."

Kevin nodded, biting his lip. "Yes. They did."

"Good. And now, instead of going off to the Western Isles, you've come to Portsmouth. It's not so nice a place, but at least you don't have to worry about elves looking down their noses at you. Welcome home." He put the book down and leaned in for a kiss.

"It does feel that way," Kevin agreed. "But I've never lived here. The closest I've been was the Isle of Wight."

"I never have either. I grew up in Worcester, about as far from the sea as I could be. But when I came here, to see the campus—it felt like home. Like old Legolas, the sound of the seabirds. Maybe in some other life…."

Kevin frowned. "You believe that stuff?"

"I'm not sure. Before I started studying hypnosis, I would've said no. Have you ever heard of hypnotic regression?"

"A little. That's used for some intelligence work—memory training, mostly."

"In hypnotherapy, it's used to get back to the original trauma that lies at the root of a problem. Whether it works is the test of whether a memory is real and significant. There've been psychiatrists, reputable ones, who had clients spontaneously regress to what sounded like earlier lives, and the regression cleared up the trouble. The doctors who've gone public about it say their colleagues tell them about other cases but won't let their names be used."

"It sounds pretty far-fetched, Johnny. Have you ever tried it yourself?"

"No. My problem was remembering too much, not the other way 'round. The way I see it, for most things it doesn't make that much difference. After all, *this* is the life that counts. The only thing that made me a little curious is what one book—Weiss, I think— says about people who have some link to one another from an earlier life. Remember what it was like when we first saw each other in that classroom?"

Kevin smiled. "Of course. True love or swine flu."

"It gave me a strange feeling when he described that sort of recognition in one of his books. The meeting of eyes. It's supposed to be the way people know when they've found each other again."

Logically, Kevin turned the idea on its head. "That would mean they'd lost each other. In some other time."

"Yeah. That was why I never looked into it. People never seem to think about it, but past-life means past-death, too. I didn't need any more death. I thought I *had* lost you, anyway. Once was enough. Now you're back, it doesn't matter one way or another. This lifetime is what we have right now, whether it's one of a string or all there is."

"Good enough. Are you ready for dessert?"

"That depends. I'd just as soon leave the cheesecake for breakfast and go back to bed." He picked up their plates, heading for the kitchen.

"You've added mind-reading to your many talents. That reminds me, you'd better not do massage and counseling together, not unless you plan to change your name."

"Why not?"

"D'you really want to be known as Dr. 'Hands-on'?"

John had not forgotten that Kevin was ticklish. By the time they'd stopped wrestling, the kittens had cleaned out the carton of coronation chicken salad.

Chapter Nine

"HERE WE are." Kevin shut off the rented van and nodded at the anonymous brick building before them. "Home sweet home." He glanced at John. "And please don't think I'm paranoid—but it's entirely possible the place is bugged now, so don't say anything you wouldn't want overheard."

Johnny looked as though he was about to say something, but he just tightened his lips and nodded. He had seemed a bit uneasy when they had been required to leave their driver's licenses at the gate. "Will they search the van before they let us leave?"

"Waste of their time. They've probably checked the apartment already. I never brought anything really personal here, Johnny—there are a few boxes at my parents' place and some papers in a safe-deposit box, or with my solicitor." Kevin shook his head. "Well, let's get on with it."

"How could you stand living under a microscope this way?" John asked as Kevin climbed into the van and started handing down the flattened packing boxes he'd bought from the van-hire agent.

"It wasn't bugged when I lived here, Johnny. I know how to make sure of that. And it's not as though I was required to live here—it was just simpler than having a flat somewhere else. No security worries, not even ordinary burglars. Besides, most of the time I didn't have enough of a personal life to care if anyone had been spying on me. In some ways it was good to know that if I vanished, someone would come looking."

"Your parents would have. So would I, if they'd told me."

"They'd have told my parents I was on a top-secret mission, and for my father, that would've been the end of it. You have no idea how Byzantine the business gets." He tossed out the last of the boxes, then caught the door handle, pulling it down as he jumped to the ground. "Come on, let's get this over with."

A few days ago, he had not been able to face the place. Now, with Johnny beside him, it seemed like years since he'd been here—just another temporary residence, a place to lay his head. Everything was as he remembered it: a short, wide flight of concrete stairs covered in a tan commercial carpet that led to the second-floor hall, his flat the second steel door on the left.

His key still opened the lock. Why was that a surprise? There'd have been no point in changing the lock and then telling him to come on ahead. But the door swung open to show everything looking as it had the morning he'd left for the hearing—quiet, orderly, and meaningless. Living room to the left, pocket kitchen to the right, bath to the left beyond that, bedroom right. It had been enough for his needs, when he'd been home at all. Now it seemed cold and alien, nothing to do with him.

John's light touch on his shoulder shook him out of his preoccupation.

"Right," Kevin said. "Let's get the boxes taped together first, then we can start filling them." He went around to the windows, pulling open the blinds to let the light in. "Or would you rather move the big stuff first?"

John shrugged. "You're right, boxes first. We'll have to clear the tops of the big things like your desk and dresser, and we'll need boxes for that."

"That's how I see it."

Kevin found it easier than he'd expected to sort and pack his possessions with John working beside him—the momentum of their activity left him no time to sit and brood. His bath towels and a spare set of sheets went into a single carton, his dress uniforms and suits into suitcases. Boxes served for everything else; the sheets that would need a wash were dumped in a laundry bag. His books took up the most space, four whole cartons.

"Still reading mysteries," John observed.

"Yeah. Sheer escapism. I think I like 'em because they're so unrealistic—they almost always have a nice, neat solution. There's a new historical series you might enjoy, after you graduate—a couple of Edwardian Cambridge dons who play detective between terms."

"I've read Sherlock Holmes," John said.

"Well, they're good puzzles—I almost never guessed the endings. And unless you believe Holmes and Watson were more than good friends, this series would have something new for you."

"Really?" If John had been a dog, his ears would have perked up.

Kevin laughed. "Really. You've got to get your nose out of the textbooks once in a while, Johnny." He realized, belatedly, that he'd done what he'd warned John not to do, said something he might not want overheard. Then that resentment kicked in again. He'd recommended a book. What of it? And if the powers-that-be were having him watched, they'd soon know all about Johnny anyway. Maybe he could give them a hint—buy one of those rainbow flags and hang it out the bedroom window.

He wondered how long this was going to last—the reflexive fear and knee-jerk anger. Then he reminded himself that the first step toward clearing that away was getting himself out of this place. He got back to work.

Another hour saw the bed knocked down, everything in boxes, and the furniture lined up beside the door like soldiers on parade. Sixteen boxes, one chest of drawers, metal bed frame and mattress set, nightstand, TV stand, portable TV, computer, a small microwave cooker, and two six-foot bookshelves. Just a little too much to fit in John's apartment and still leave them room to walk. It was a pity they hadn't had time to look for a new place.

"Ready to start loading?" John asked. "I'll go get the trolley."

"We don't need that."

"Your arm," John said simply. "I won't be a minute."

Irritated, Kevin caught hold of one of the bookcases, intending to pick it up and follow John out to the van—and nearly dropped it as a pain shot up his bicep and into his shoulder, draining the strength from his right hand.

Odd. He hadn't noticed any problems while they were packing.

Of course he hadn't. There hadn't been any problems. John had unobtrusively arranged matters so that every time Kevin filled a packing box, Johnny was right there to hand him another empty one and take the full box away. And they had moved all the furniture together—none of that was especially massive.

Kevin laughed ruefully. No point in exercising his temper on Johnny for being so thoughtful. "All right, damn it," he said aloud.

"What?" John said, rattling in with the handcart.

"Nothing. You're right. Thanks."

John grinned. "I want you healed up and fit when we have to move my things. Top floor, remember?"

"Ah, an ulterior motive."

"Of course. I had to carry everything up there by myself." He shook his head at Kevin's look of consternation. "It was easier than you'd think. The mattress was the hardest, and that was just awkward. Everything else comes apart, and I bought the futon with a free delivery offer."

"Using your brains instead of your back."

"Not today." John waggled the handcart. "Shall we?"

"Just a minute." Kevin found the box with first-aid supplies and fished out an elastic bandage. "If I'm going to be sensible instead of butch, you'd better give me a hand with this." It probably wasn't necessary, but he didn't want to drop any furniture on John.

Johnny took the bandage, stretching a length between his hands, his eyes sparking with mischief. "Did you say 'sensible' or sensu—"

"Just wrap the arm!" Kevin said quickly.

Laughing, John complied.

Like the rest of the task, the loading went quickly, and they had decided to drive past John's flat—"*Our* flat," Johnny corrected—to offload Kevin's clothing and swap his larger television for John's. That meant leaving those few items to be loaded in last, and there was nothing left but one carton and a suitcase when they returned to the flat for the last time.

"I'll check the cupboards," John said, stepping into the kitchen. "Just to make sure."

Kevin did a quick walk-through of the rest of the flat. His mother had trained him to sweep up when he moved out, but this was one time he was going to disregard her instruction. Someone would be coming in to clean the place anyway, no matter what he did; when he'd arrived, it had felt and even smelled like a hotel. That hadn't changed.

His footsteps echoed hollowly. Bedroom empty. Closet empty, even the upper shelves. Bath, linen cupboard… all empty, all clear.

Hardly surprising. He hadn't really had a life here anyway. It had just been a place to sleep. "Let's go, Johnny," he said, catching hold of the suitcase with his left hand. "It's a long drive home."

THEY WERE lazy again and had dinner out on the way home after dropping off the rental van. It was getting on to ten, a bit late, but Kevin picked the Spice Island Inn and said he was paying in a tone that brooked no argument. They were shown to a table on the second floor, right beside a big window with a view of the lights glittering on the water and the big liners gliding silently along on their way to warm, sunny places like Spain and Greece. They looked like floating Travel Inns, with tourists standing at the rails, gazing back at the lights of Portsmouth.

"Would you like to go on a cruise sometime, Johnny?" Kevin asked, looking up from the menu. "Something really posh, maybe for a honeymoon?"

John was considering the menu's prices. "Not until I have a job, at least," he said, and then what Kevin had said penetrated his awareness. "Honeymoon?" There weren't many people in the dining room; John thought his voice had been terribly loud, but no one seemed to notice. "Kev," he said, more quietly, "are you saying '*like*' a honeymoon, or—"

Kevin looked up almost shyly. "Yes, I'm saying a honeymoon. Johnny, we can get a civil partnership now, make it official. We could even get married in London, if you like. My mother would be thrilled." John was speechless, and Kevin hesitated. "Too soon, isn't it? Sorry. You don't need to answer right now. We ought to take it slow, live together for a while before we jump into it."

Looking into Kevin's eyes, John didn't feel like waiting ten minutes. But he knew Kevin was right. And how many case studies had he read that showed the stupidity of rushing something this important? "I don't feel it's too soon, but I want to make it right. We have the rest of our lives. Kev. I know what I want. I suppose it does make more sense to give it some time, to be sure we can still make it work."

"I know. But this is what I want, Johnny." He looked calmer than he had that night he'd appeared on John's doorstep, calm and content. "I want you. A sane life. A real home of our own. I've never been as happy, as complete, if you like, as I was those months we were together. I want that back, and this time I want to keep it."

"So do I." He wanted very badly to just lean across the table and kiss Kevin, but legal rights or not, he wasn't ready to handle a shouting match with some drunken yob. He settled for reaching across the table, his hand partly hidden by the menu. "Whenever you want, love. But let's take time to decide where we want to honeymoon. And I do need to graduate first."

Kevin's hand was warm. "Of course. We'll have to sort out jobs, too. Will you need to do a term as a house officer?"

"Yes. I'm set up with a local counseling center. It's scheduled to begin right after the holidays, though, New Year's week. I could postpone it until the first of February, or even cancel if you get a position somewhere else, but it's probably best if I go into one as soon as I can so I don't forget everything I've learned."

"So long as you remember the maths until Tuesday."

"My God, it's Sunday already, isn't it? There's only tomorrow to study—"

"And we'll be sleeping in late," Kevin said with an evil grin.

"We will?" That grin sent a message right down to John's groin, and heat flushed through him. "If we'd had anything more for lunch than a couple of apples, I'd drag you home right now."

"Don't we still have some leftovers?" Kevin asked.

But the waitress was already there with her list of the evening's special dishes. She smiled indulgently at their joined hands and asked what they'd like for dinner. It was nearly two hours, a big meal, and a bottle of champagne later that they dragged each other up the stairs to their flat.

Their flat. "Who carries who over the threshold?" Kevin asked as John fumbled for the key. "Whom, I mean."

"We carry each other," John decided. "All for one, one for all."

Horatio and Emma—they'd given up and gone historical— were squalling at them as soon as the door swung open, and they had their hands full keeping the kittens from escaping. Kevin made sure their water bowls and kibble were replenished while John dished up two saucers of canned kitten food.

"This having kits is serious business," Kevin said, and snickered. "What happens when they grow up and ask for the car keys?"

"Doesn't matter," John said. "They won't get far. No opposable thumbs, they can't turn the ignition." He tossed the cat food tin in the bin and wrapped his arms around Kevin, pulling his lover against him as he leaned back against the sink. "Damn it, Kev, I'm so fucking glad you came back."

Kevin's lips met his, and he lost himself in the kiss—such a strange expression, if you'd never done it, but he was just this side of drunk, and somehow it became easy to lose track of where he ended and Kevin began. Heat, warmth, closeness—the inexpressible safety of knowing that he could reach out and count on Kevin being there, that the edges of their separate, lonely selves would match and join into something bigger… and even more, the urgent hunger in his body meeting its match as their cocks rubbed together through their jeans.

He tried to draw back as Kevin rocked against him more urgently. "Bed?"

"Why?"

Good question. Why bother? They'd get there eventually, and he was so fuzzy with champagne and hot with this beautiful man in his arms that he just let it all flow. Kevin was back. He was staying. *Forever now, thought you were dead, oh God I love you love you love you—*

John slumped against Kevin's shoulder and heard him say, "Looks as though it's laundry time," and startled Kevin by picking him up bodily and staggering off to the bedroom.

KEVIN FOUND himself being nudged awake by something bumping into his face. He ignored it as long as he could—he didn't want to wake up yet—but it wouldn't stop. Finally he batted at the irritation and felt fur... and heard a faint rumbling.

He opened one eye to see Emma's pink nose and mad baby eyes only an inch away, one tiny paw raised to pat his chin once more. "Look, you little pest—" She squeaked a response, and he guessed it must be breakfast time, whether he liked it or not.

He didn't much feel like moving, with Johnny curled comfortably against his back, but as he surrendered to the inevitable and began to stretch, he realized he was still wearing his shoes.

And his jeans. And everything else. And Horatio was chewing on his shoelaces. "Oh, for God's sake," Kevin said. One bottle of champagne split between them shouldn't have knocked them both flat. But it had been a long day, up early and home late, and that last enthusiastic shag in the kitchen had just done him in. He remembered Johnny dumping him onto the bed, then snuggling up beside him—and nothing beyond that.

But, amazingly, he had slept through the night, and without nightmares. He hadn't wakened in a panic when the kitten nudged him. And even though he hadn't been able to sleep in as long as he'd have liked, he actually felt rested. "Johnny?"

John pulled a pillow over his head and muttered something negative.

"Your cats are starving, you lazy sod. And we need a shower." Kevin stripped out of his jeans and went into the kitchen to deal with the clamoring throng. He started water for tea, had a quick shave, and caught the pot just as the whistle began to sing. Eggs and sausage, that sounded like a good start.

When he got back, John was snoring. Kevin watched him for a moment, teetering between affection and exasperation. Adopting those cats had been Johnny's idea, after all, but who was it getting up to feed them? And there was another chore that went with cats— the dreaded litter pan. "Fair enough, chum," he said. "If I have to feed them, you know who's assigned to latrine duty."

No response from the insensate lump. Exasperation got the upper hand. "John, it's nearly nine a.m. Wakey-wakey." He rolled Johnny over, unzipped his lover's jeans, pulled off his shoes, and had him bare-assed before he knew what was going on.

"Kevin, what the hell—?"

"Time to get up!" Kevin pulled off his own shirt and tugged at John's cotton sweater, dragging it up and over his head. "We're filthy, and you have work to do."

"We don't have to get up immediately, do we?" John caught hold of him, pulling him down and wrapping his legs around Kevin's. "I thought you said we were going to sleep in."

"I've been up for hours." Kevin thought a bit of exaggeration was fair, all things considered. "I don't know why those little beggars pick on me to feed them—you're their mummy."

"What?" John wriggled against him suggestively. "Does that feel like a mother cat?"

If they hadn't both been so grubby, Kevin might've succumbed. "It feels like we need a shower. I stink, and so do you. And then we hit the books."

"Together?" John asked hopefully. He was really too damned alluring, still sleepy-eyed and tousled, with a faint shadow of beard coming in.

"The books? Sure, I said I'd help you study."

"No, the shower." John rubbed his face against Kevin's chest. "Mmm. You do smell." He nuzzled the side of Kevin's neck, sending a shiver through him. "You smell sexy. I like it." There was a purr in his voice that reminded Kevin of the kittens. And given another minute, Johnny would get his way, just as they had done.

But Kevin knew perfectly well that if they dove back into the blankets, they might stay there all day, and even though he would have preferred to do exactly that, he knew John was just avoiding his textbooks. "Up," he said, rolling away with regret. "Duty calls. After you've passed that exam with flying colors, we can stay in bed till noon if you like."

"Are you trying to bribe me with sexual favors?" John demanded.

"Damn, you're perceptive. And I've got something new… while you took the kittens to the vet, I went out and found a new lube that's supposed to be waterproof. Thought it might be fun to try in the shower." He gathered up the dirty clothes and headed for the bathroom, dropping them in the laundry basket on the way.

"If it's waterproof, how do you wash it off?" John asked, tagging along behind him.

"Soap."

"Ah." John ducked into the tiny stall and started the water, adjusting the taps until it was comfortable. "Come on in, love. Got your goodies?"

"Yeah, and the lube, too." Kevin had also brought some shower gel along from his old place, lemon-scented stuff that had always reminded him of the summer he and John had lived together. It would be pleasant here in the summer, with the ocean breeze blowing cool air in off the water.

In the meantime, he put the containers on the built-in shelf so he could give his full attention to Johnny. They washed each other's hair first—always easier to have that out of the way. The showerhead was barely high enough to do the job, and Kevin kept banging his elbows on the translucent walls. "This stall was designed for pygmies, wasn't it?"

"It was designed for one pygmy," Johnny said. "C'mere." He pulled Kevin close so their foreheads touched, and angled him under the water. "Hold still."

As Johnny's fingers worked the shampoo into his scalp, Kevin relaxed. This had to be heaven. John tipped his head back just a little more and began kissing him, slowly and carefully, as if they had all the time in the world, tongue sliding between Kevin's lips in a teasing way. His hands wandered off for a moment, and then Kevin caught the tang of lemon as John started washing his back, from the neck down, long circular swirls on either side of his spine, all the way down to his bum. Touching but not gripping… just enough to start a slow burn.

And in front, of course, his cock was rubbing against John's in that same gentle, tantalizing rhythm. He was just starting to put a little effort into the movement when John moved his kisses to the side of Kevin's neck, easing him around under the shower spray.

Kevin gasped as the water spattered against his chest and belly, and again when John reached around and began soaping him in front, from the throat down. It wasn't really necessary to wash his nipples so thoroughly, but *damn*, it felt good.

As Johnny's hands moved down his chest and lower, Kevin reached behind himself to grip his lover's thighs. He had to touch John somewhere; it would've been against their unwritten rules for Kevin to touch himself and hurry things along. So he held on to John and let his head drop back, enjoying the promise of that hot cock along the cleft of his arse and the knowing hands in front, as Johnny lathered him up all the way down to his balls. And finally, when he was just about ready to scream, that warm, wet hand closed around his cock.

"You ready?" John murmured.

Kevin couldn't manage anything more coherent than a long, drawn-out groan. He let go of John long enough to fumble for the lube and get some of it out of the tube and into himself. It would've been easier if John had stopped what he was doing, but he had the rhythm and it was worth any inconvenience to keep that long, slow glide of pleasure.

Then he felt Johnny's fingers slip in from behind. He bent forward, bracing himself against the side of the stall and hoping it would hold. He relaxed as John pressed into him, letting his body open to take that hot, smooth shaft. The water, the scents, the moisture rising all around him…. Kevin loved the rough-and-tumble of sex in bed—or on the sofa, or up against the kitchen wall. There wasn't any kind of sex with Johnny he didn't enjoy. But if he had to pick a favorite, it would be the full sensory delight of making love in the shower.

Not that he had time to consider the matter so coherently. It wasn't until he felt Johnny holding him almost still with an arm around his waist that he realized the shower stall was actually starting to shake with the force of their movements. But he couldn't stop, he couldn't, he was so close—and then he was there, over the edge, as Johnny thrust into him one final time and his own body shuddered with release.

They stood there panting for a few seconds. Then Kevin turned in Johnny's arms and kissed him again, too out of breath to speak.

"Anorexic pygmies," John said finally. "Too flimsy for us to do anything but have a wash without destroying the plumbing. We need to find a better bathroom, Kev."

"I'll call the estate agent while you're taking that exam," Kevin agreed. He brushed his lips against Johnny's very gently. "Now, if I'm not mistaken, you have an appointment with a statistics review. You go organize your books while I fry us up some breakfast."

"Slave driver."

"Absolutely. How do you want your eggs?"

Chapter Ten

"KEVIN!" JOHN propped his bicycle in the narrow space under the stair. He caught himself, surprised at the echo from his shout, then realized the other tenants probably weren't home at three in the afternoon anyway, so he galloped up the three flights without worrying about the noise. "Kevin! I passed!"

Kevin looked up from the card table they'd crammed into one corner of the living room. "Brilliant! How do you know?"

"Professor Krieger grades exams on the spot for graduating seniors. There were only three of us." He leaned over Kevin, managing a quick hug and a peek at the estate listings spread across the table. "It hasn't sunk in yet that I'm through with classes, but I'll cope. Anything promising?"

"A few. How did you do? Did you keep your head on the confidence intervals?"

"I did! And I aced standard deviations. I left off everything about our nonstandard sort." That earned him a grin and a kiss. "I totally screwed up on the type-one, type-two errors. That was the worst of it, though, and there wasn't much of that anyway. I won't graduate with high honors, but it should be cum laude. This was the hardest class I ever took." He looked around for the kittens, who were nowhere to be seen. "Have you fed the wild creatures?"

"I did, yes. They were chasing each other around like maniacs until I rattled the kibble. They're sleeping it off now."

"Thanks." John poured himself a glass of water and glanced around, slightly hungry. "Apple?"

"Sure."

"So what've you found?" John asked as he ducked into the fridge and snagged a pair of apples. He brought them over, putting one down on the papers and rubbing his free hand along Kevin's back. He enjoyed the feel of Kevin's muscles under the light sweater. Every time John touched him, it was a wonderful living proof of what had been restored to him.

"Mmm." Kevin leaned into the caress and let his head drop back; John leaned down to kiss him. After a moment, Kevin disengaged and said, "Two that look fairly standard—they might be worth checking. But there's one I think we should see right away. It has a lease with option to buy after the first year."

"That sounds pretty permanent." John frowned at the listing, which didn't seem to have that information included.

"No commitment for a year, though—and that should be enough time for us to see if we want to stay here. I called the estate agent's and looked at a few pictures on their website. It's a townhouse, belongs to an older couple who got tired of Portsmouth winters and moved to Spain. They wanted to hedge their bets in case they can't get used to all that lovely warm weather, so they decided not to sell immediately. Whoever rents it gets first refusal on buying in a year's time." He crunched into the apple. "If it's as good as it sounds, I think we'll like it."

"What's the attraction?"

Kevin glanced up, teasing. "Let's just look at it first. I'd like to see what you think. If we want it, though, we'll need to jump on it. I've made an appointment with the agent."

"Today?"

"In half an hour, if you're up for it."

John sighed. "I was hoping to be up for something else—" And he would be later, no doubt. But Kevin seemed to be up to something himself. His eyes were bright with anticipation and his excitement was contagious. "All right, let's go."

They drove, although they probably could have made it on foot in half an hour. The property had a tiny one-car garage included at the back and a smallish garden. "I like it so far," John said. "But the rent is steep."

"A bit more than twice what you're paying," Kevin said. "I know, it is high. But there'll be two of us paying. And if we were to buy, they'd let us apply half the rent toward a down payment. It could be a great investment, Johnny." He nodded at the figure in a trench coat standing at the front steps. "There's the agent, I think."

The agent, a middle-aged blond woman, introduced herself as Mrs. Bell and let them into the place. Like so many townhouses, it was narrow, sandwiched between two similar buildings. Its tiny vestibule had an archway to the left into what looked like a living room, with a hall to the right and a stairway against the far right wall. "The kitchen is at the back," she said, leading them in. "It's an open floor plan from the kitchen through to the living room. I think the owners made very clever use of the space."

They had indeed. The place had been remodeled with an eye to function without trying to modernize it too far. The kitchen and dining room took up the rear half of the ground floor, and in the dining room, a set of sliding doors opened to a view across a small deck and into the back garden. Toward the front, the dining area flowed into the bright, high-ceilinged living room, where a wide front window looked onto the street.

"The owners did most of the upgrading themselves," Mrs. Bell said. "He's a retired builder. I suppose this was his busman's holiday."

"Nice," Kevin said, and John had to agree. He didn't think much of the mushroom design all over the kitchen wallpaper, but he had been Gran's paint-and-paper man for the last eight years of her life. He could deal with wallpaper easily enough. The kitchen was, all by itself, nearly as big as their current flat's living room, and a tiny powder room had been tucked into a corner by the dining room. That would be handy if they had friends over. And to top it all off, beside the powder room was a combination washer-dryer. The place really had everything they could have hoped for.

"There's a cellar too," Mrs. Bell said. "Nothing special, and it's a bit dusty, so it would be best to see upstairs first—" Her handbag suddenly burst into a tinny version of the "Ride of the Valkyries." "Oh, sorry, I meant to mute my phone."

"Why don't you take your call?" Kevin suggested as she fished the device out of her handbag. "We can have a look upstairs by ourselves."

"Thanks, dear."

He smiled at her and nodded toward the stair. "What do you think so far?" he asked as they ascended.

"I like it," John said. "More posh than I'm used to, of course. We don't really need anything this fancy, do we?"

"Need? No. But if we were to buy it and then move after a few years, I'm sure we could sell for a profit, or even lease it out ourselves. Here's the master bedroom."

The owners had done a decent job. The room had a snug double-pane window that would keep out the street noises. It also had an alcove that had probably been intended either as a nursery or a maid's room, a tiny space only about three meters by two. The other bedroom, at the back, was about the size of the first, but its window overlooked the garden.

"I think I'd rather use this as our room," John said. "It would be quieter—and we could use the other as office space or a guest room." But he was still not convinced they needed it. There was no way he'd be able to carry his full share of the expense of a two-story house.

"Here's what I wanted to show you," Kevin said. "The owner... well, he wasn't a builder, exactly—"

Kevin opened the door to what had to be the bath, and John laughed in delight as he stepped inside. "They liked their mod cons, didn't they?"

"Either that, or he tested new products here. Mrs. Bell told me his business was selling and installing plumbing fixtures. This is why the rent's so steep. It's a masterpiece, isn't it? The online pictures didn't do it justice."

The bathroom was a sybarite's delight, done in tones of blue and white that reminded him of a sunny day at the seashore. Tiny, irregular tiles on the floor mimicked the look of a pebbly beach. Instead of a tub across one side of the room, there was a corner spa tub with room enough for two to sit, and whirlpool jets inside it. Between tub and shower was a towel-warming rack, and the shower itself—what a project that must have been! One side of it curved around, with the entire surface inside and out covered in tiny iridescent glass tiles.

John stepped inside, amazed at the effect. It was beautiful, like being inside a seashell. "No door?"

"Look at the design," Kevin said. "With the shower head where it is, all the water stays inside. You don't need a door, or even a curtain. It's the same idea as the one in the gym back at the training center, only smaller and a lot more private."

They had often fantasized about making use of the gym shower back in officers' training, but neither of them was an exhibitionist; common sense or cowardice had kept them from ever actually attempting it. But here—this little grotto had plenty of room for both of them, and even a couple of handy grab bars.

"No worry about ripping this plumbing out of the wall!" John said happily. He took a firm grip on one of the bars and shot Kevin a look of invitation. "Do you suppose she'd let us test it?"

"Probably not both together," Kevin said with such regret that John laughed again.

"But…." He had been living frugally for so long he had to ask. "Can we really afford this?"

"I have a lot of vacation pay saved up, Johnny." Kevin ruffled his lover's hair. "Yes, we can afford it. I can't think of a better use for the money. In fact, I've been saving for a down payment on a place—renting is just pouring money down a hole." Then, demonstrating that the shower design provided considerable privacy even if Mrs. Bell should come upstairs, he pulled John's face down for a kiss.

The idea of what this would be like with both of them naked and wet sent John's imagination racing to a place he couldn't let it linger. He pulled back, shaking his head and grinning. "You ought to ask this agency for a job. You've got a quite a sales pitch."

Kevin let go reluctantly. "I'm sorry if I seem bloody-minded about this, Johnny. I may be rushing things a bit. But this is a real opportunity, and the one-year lease would give us plenty of time to decide whether it's the right place to settle down. If we find we hate it for some reason, or one of us finds a better job elsewhere, it shouldn't be difficult to sublet."

"I'm sure you're right." John looked around the sparkling room, with its space-age comforts. "I don't know why it seems to loom so large—I know the commitment is really just a year, the same as we'd be considering anywhere else. It's just so much change so fast—I'm still half expecting to wake up and find none of this is real."

Kevin shook his head, one side of his mouth quirking upward. "I feel as though I've been having a long, rotten dream and I just woke up. But if you're not ready—"

"I seem to remember being the one who said you should move in. Maybe I'm just surprised at it all coming together so quickly." John touched the beautiful tile, wondering why he was unable to share in Kevin's enthusiasm. Was it some sort of guilt on his part? It was hardly as though their having a comfortable home would take anything away from people elsewhere in the world, whose homes had been bombed out. There were other things he could do if he wanted to help with war relief.

And Kev had been through the grinder himself, battered by war even if he didn't see it that way. If Kevin needed a place to come home to, a place where he'd feel secure, what right did John have to deny him that? "All right," he said. "As you say, it's only a year's commitment, and it sounds as though you know more about this sort of thing than I do."

"Mainly by osmosis," Kevin said. "My father didn't make his fortune in the Army, you know. He dabbled in real estate all along, and went into it full-time when he retired. I don't know half what he does—but I do know Portsmouth property isn't cheap, and this place is a plum. There are bound to be problems—there always are—but we'll have time to find them before we commit ourselves."

"Mr. Kendrick?" Mrs. Bell's voice floated up the stair. "I have another client who'd like to come by and view this home. Would you like to see the cellar now?"

Kevin stepped out of the shower. "Yes, we'll be right down," he called, and turned back to John, the question clear as day in his blue eyes.

Some risks were worth taking. John gave his lover a quick pat on the bum. "All right. It's only a year. Let's see if she's brought the forms with her. We don't want someone else pinching our house."

"BACK UP!"

Kevin stopped immediately, balancing the corner of the box spring on his knee. "What's wrong?"

"Just back up!" Johnny sounded almost angry, so Kevin did as he demanded. "Sorry," he said in a calmer tone. "My hand was caught between the box and the door frame. Tilt it a little to the left—no, sorry, my left, your right."

Kevin did as instructed, and their cumbersome burden cleared the front door on the second attempt.

"Let's just take it on up," John called.

"Okay." He had to guess at where Johnny was—there was no seeing around the bulky object—and simply kept his end up as it angled through the door, which swung shut, locking behind him. The mattress had been even clumsier to handle, but for sheer aggravation, he gave the futon frame top marks. The damned thing had kept trying to unfold itself all the way up the stairs. It would be useful, though, in what they were calling the library—comfortable enough for lounging and a private guest room if they should have overnight visitors.

This house had room enough for all the furniture they intended to keep, and Kevin was quietly pleased at how easily their belongings had combined. His own bed had not been a keeper; he'd had that mattress since university. John's mattress set had turned out to be much newer and a lot more comfortable. Kevin's living room furniture suited the size of the new place, and they had distributed their existing bookshelves throughout the house and had bought three full-size ones, now in their cartons up in the library, waiting for assembly. Kevin's mother was delighted to know she'd be able to clear out the books they'd been storing for him, as well as the four-poster bed inherited from his grandparents that she had insisted he would want someday.

And despite Johnny's dislike of what he called the fungal wallpaper in the kitchen, they hadn't needed to do anything major to the new place. Their landlords had left basic blinds and curtains, nothing special but enough for now, for privacy. Eventually they would have to find a proper dining table and a few decent chairs, but for the moment, the card table and folding chairs would do well enough.

It was a good thing they had sit-down room in the kitchen. In their excitement over the gorgeous spa bathroom, they'd overlooked the fact that there was no ceiling fixture at all in the dining area. They'd have to find a couple of lamps or see if the parents had any old ones knocking around the attic, and eventually they'd want a ceiling light. But the house was all coming together. Another week and they'd be settled in as comfortably as if those years apart had never happened.

"Stop," Johnny said. "Just set it down on the top step."

"What's wrong?"

His head appeared around the other side of the box. "Nothing, just had to change my grip. Shall we take it right on in to the bedroom and put it on the frame?"

"Why not?"

Johnny nodded, then gave Kevin an affectionate smile. "I can't get over how much easier this all is with someone to carry the other end of the furniture."

The unconcealed joy in his voice touched Kevin to the heart, but he knew if he responded in kind, they'd never get the job done. He'd never tried shagging on a stair with a mattress between, and this was no time to make the experiment. "Yes it is," he said, "but this is the heavy end, so if you could move it, please?"

"Oh, sorry."

Two minutes later the bed was assembled—blankets, pillows, duvet and all.

"That looks awfully inviting," Kevin said.

John threw an arm around him, making the invitation stronger with the scent rising from his body. "But it's not on the Master Plan. Don't tempt me."

"I know. Work first, sweets later." He was naughty enough to pull John into a thorough kiss, savoring the salty tang of honest sweat.

"It's a good thing we took the edge off this morning," John gasped.

"Let's get moving, then. We have to return the van by four."

They had spent the previous night here with nothing but a six-pack of beer and the mattress on the floor, and started the day with a shower and good clean fun in what Johnny was calling Neptune's Grotto. They'd promised themselves a decadent evening in the tub if they were able to finish the move in good time.

They really did make an effective team, and the two weeks between applying for the lease and the final approval had given Kevin's arm time to finish healing. John had insisted on wrapping it, just as a precaution, but it had given Kevin no trouble. One final load of small things from the old flat—television and stereo, food from the fridge—and they were ready to go fetch the kittens from the vet's office and call it a night.

"Do you want to make it all one trip?" John asked as they locked the door behind them for the last time and got into the car.

"I don't see what good that would do," Kevin said. "Where were you planning to put them? There's no room in the backseat or on your lap, and if you put that carrier between us, I can't shift gears."

John peered into the overloaded backseat. "I see your point."

"Besides, the vet's in the opposite direction. They'll yowl if we leave them in the cage while we unload, and if we don't, they'll be underfoot or out in the street."

John laughed. "I hear you, Kev. Note to self: Kevin does not enjoy driving with cats."

"Sorry," Kevin said. "But I never expected that god-awful racket."

"They did put up a screech, didn't they? I didn't expect that—they were so quiet when we first picked them up."

"They were probably just weak from hunger," Kevin said, trying to sound grumpy but not doing too good a job. He'd expected to grit his teeth and put up with cramming the carrier into the overcrowded vehicle. He was getting spoiled, no doubt about it—Johnny really seemed to enjoy caring for him, adjusting to make Kevin's life easier.

And John's next words proved it once again. "Tell you what, love, if you fix dinner, I'll go get the monsters."

"Will you settle for spaghetti?"

"I'll settle for frozen pizza, so long as you bake it first. In fact, I'll settle for anything you want to feed me." Johnny's hand crept suggestively across the space between the seats.

"Not while I'm driving, you randy devil," Kevin warned. "There's no room for that either. I vote for pizza, then. No washing-up afterward."

"Not dishes, anyway."

"Well, no. But after all this manual labor, I'm sure we'll need a bath."

"Oh, yes. Absolutely."

With that prospect ahead of them, it took only a few minutes to get the last bits out of the car and settled in around the house. The television went on its stand, and John's portable stereo just fit on a low shelf between the living and dining rooms. When that was done, John closed the curtains and turned on a lamp before coming back for a kiss.

"I'll go get the animals, then. Is there anything you want me to pick up while I'm—"

The shrill ring of the phone in the kitchen echoed loudly in the hall; they both jumped.

"That's not supposed to be hooked up," Kevin said, heading for the kitchen more or less by reflex.

"It wouldn't be the first time a shut-off order got ignored," John said after another couple of rings. "Probably a wrong number, anyway."

"I suppose." Kevin shrugged. Whoever was calling was certainly persistent. "You're probably right. Let's set them straight and send them on their way." He reached over and picked up the receiver. "Hello?"

"Kendrick. Glad I caught you."

The shock left him momentarily speechless. He shot John a startled look and covered the receiver. "Hang on a minute, Johnny."

"What is it?"

"Trouble."

KEVIN FORCED his voice to neutrality. "Hello, Colonel. I've moved, as you're clearly aware. What's going on? Some forms I forgot to sign?"

"There's no problem with your paperwork, Kendrick. Never has been. I'm calling to tell you to be careful."

For a moment Kevin found himself speechless. "It's a bit late for that, isn't it?" he finally managed.

His commanding officer—no, make that *former* CO—sounded testy. "Kendrick, this is serious. You may be in danger."

"What, my resignation wasn't enough? Is someone in some ministry or other out for my blood?"

"Goddamn it, Kendrick, I'm in no mood for jokes!"

Kevin wasn't either, but he did have a degree of respect for the Colonel. Not as much as he'd once had, but.... "Can you be a little more specific, sir?"

"Not very. Do you remember Major Shaney?"

"Of course." Major Shaney. Who had given the all clear to hand over the prisoners—after the debacle—and then denied having done so after the shit hit the fan. Major Don't-Turn-Your-Back-On-Him Shaney.

"He's dead. Hit-and-run, yesterday evening. A stolen car, found abandoned a few miles from the scene. No fingerprints or other evidence."

No loss. Kevin didn't say it. He didn't want to be considered a suspect, though he had at least three witnesses who could place him in Portsmouth the previous evening. No, five—three humans and two cats. "I hope you're not taking up a collection?"

"We think it may be related to the incident."

The incident. Christ, couldn't he just say it? Kevin closed his eyes and counted to ten. "Sir, I'm out of the game. What exactly is it you expect of me?"

"Officially, nothing. Are you armed?"

What? "No, of course not. I'm a civilian now, remember?" That wasn't the whole truth; "armed" was a broad term, and there were half a dozen items with lethal potential within easy reach, thanks to his thorough training. But the Colonel knew that.

"You're on a consultant contract as of now. Expect a delivery sometime between eight p.m. and midnight. You'll receive weapons and a special carry permit, plus security hardware for your residence."

"I haven't signed any contract yet," Kevin said. "And I don't intend to until you at least tell me who or what I'm supposed to be watching for."

He waited while the Colonel digested his new attitude. "We have intelligence that the mercenaries involved in the incident were dismissed but not charged. We think one or more may be involved with Shaney's death. We know some of them are in the States, but there are several we haven't tracked yet. We have reason to believe at least one of them may be here in the UK."

"I see."

"Good. I've had an emergency number downloaded to your mobile phone. You can reach it on speed dial number five."

Son of a bitch. "Yeah, all right," Kevin said. He glanced up at Johnny, who had moved a little closer and stood watching him with a worried expression. "Colonel, would it be better for me to get out of the country for a while?"

John shook his head, mouthing "No," and it seemed his former CO agreed with him.

"Absolutely not. We can cover you more effectively if you remain in England. Are you planning to stay where you are for now?"

What, you haven't read my mind? "I was. As I'm sure you know, I just signed a lease. But I'll clear out if necessary. I'm not going to bring this kind of trouble on my friends." He held up a hand, willing Johnny to keep quiet for just a minute longer.

"We don't know for certain this has anything to do with you," the Colonel said. "No need to panic."

Kevin didn't dignify that with an answer.

After a moment of silence, the Colonel said, "You probably won't believe me, Captain, but I am sorry this has come up. We all appreciate what you did, and this has caught us all by surprise. I'll keep you informed as the situation develops. Call if you have any questions or if you notice anything suspicious."

"I will." He was about to end the call when a thought struck him. "Colonel, am I under surveillance?"

"Six men, eight-hour rotations. They'll be moving into position across the street this evening."

The thought grew to a suspicion. "No electronics in this flat," Kevin said.

"Are you giving me an order?"

"I'm telling you there is no *need to know* the details of my personal life, Colonel." He met Johnny's eyes and held the look as he laid down the law in a way he'd never have dared when he was in the service. "As you've no doubt concluded, I have a lover. My lover is a man. Our private lives are just that. If we decide to have sex in the bedroom or on the sofa or hanging from the chandelier or anywhere else *in our home*, nobody needs to listen in. Nobody needs to know if one of us snores."

The Colonel practically sputtered. "That's not—"

Kevin grinned humorlessly. "We both know how boring surveillance can get, don't we, Colonel? How often the boys just get curious and turn up the gain a little bit to find out what folks are up to in bed? I'd sooner be shot dead than turn up in an MP3 in Peabody's gag file. I had my fifteen minutes of fame at the hearing, and I don't want any more."

A moment of silence, then, "Understood."

"Thank you." Could he trust the man's word? Not likely. "Colonel? I'm going to do a fine-tooth comb of this flat. If I find any surveillance equipment—and you know I will, if there's anything to find—I'm going to put the thing in the oven and set it to broil. Is that clear?"

"That's unreasonable, Kendrick."

"But it wouldn't be *your* equipment, would it, sir? Tell you what. I'll let you bug my bedroom if you let me bug yours." That was a low blow; rumor had it that the Colonel and his wife slept in separate rooms.

"Damn it—"

"This is not a standard operation," Kevin said, fed up with the deception. "You can't feed me the bullshit you give the civilians. Do you want to catch the killer?"

"Yes. But I don't want any more casualties."

"Neither do I. And I know enough about the risks to make my own informed decisions. How will the shipment arrive?"

"In a furniture truck. It's packaged as exercise equipment. Are we in agreement, then?"

"I suppose so. One other thing—body armor, two sets. I'm sure you know the sizes."

"That's already included. Thanks for your cooperation, Kendrick. With any luck, I'll be calling you soon to let you know to stand down."

"I'll be waiting." Kevin looked at his watch. "In fact, I'll give your team an hour, right now, to clean the place out. Just in case anyone got overzealous and left some equipment here that doesn't belong."

"I'll see to it that your privacy is respected. Good-bye, Captain."

"It isn't 'captain' anymore," Kevin reminded him. "Good-bye." He hung the phone up carefully, controlling the urge to tear it off the wall and throw it out the window.

"What's going on?" Johnny asked. "You're not leaving again." It wasn't a question.

"I can't talk about it yet. Not here. Let's go for a ride, Johnny." He dug out his car keys and tossed them over. "You drive."

He knew it was most likely his imagination that made a spot between his shoulder blades itch when they went out onto the street. And he knew he looked like a fool when he raised the bonnet, and even more so when he got down to check beneath the car before taking the keys and starting it himself. That didn't matter. He wasn't about to take chances with Johnny's life. He left the keys in the ignition and climbed into the passenger side.

"Kev, where are we going?" John asked, once they were clear of the car park and rolling down the road. "What the hell is going on?"

"I need to get out of the house for a little while. Let's go grocery shopping." That wasn't just a way of killing time either, come to think of it. If this was going to turn into a siege, now was the time to lay in provisions.

"What?"

"Bear with me, please." Kevin put a hand on Johnny's thigh, felt the tension in his body. It wasn't fair to throw him into this. "I'll explain everything, I promise."

John put his hand over Kevin's. "All right. Mind if I switch on the radio?"

"No, go ahead." They drove another ten minutes to the sprightly but incongruous melodies of a Strauss waltz festival while Kevin checked the number now programmed into his mobile phone, noted it on a page of his pocket notebook, then pulled the back of the phone off and disconnected the battery. While he had the notebook out, he started a grocery list.

Halfway through "The Blue Danube," John turned into the car park at Tesco's and stopped the car at the edge of the lot, far away from the building. "All right, now can you—"

Kevin put a finger to his lips and got out of the car. John followed, frowning. When they were a few yards away from the vehicle, Kevin stopped. "Johnny, I'm sorry. I couldn't be sure the car isn't bugged."

"Never mind apologizing, I can see it's not your idea. Just tell me what's going on."

Kevin outlined the situation, with a few heartfelt expletives thrown in for good measure. "And they've taken it upon themselves to add an emergency number to my phone." He tore out the page and gave it to John. "Keep this. If anything happens to me, or if we get separated and you see anything suspicious, call that number."

John tucked the page in his pocket. "What did you do to your mobile?"

"I took the battery out. That shuts off the fucking GPS and keeps them from eavesdropping on us."

"What?"

"Think about it. Mobile phones bounce their signals off satellites—that's how global positioning works, right?"

"Yes. Oh." John's eyes widened. "Damn! That's right—remote location for emergencies. Last year some lost hikers were rescued because one of them had a mobile phone."

"Right. Most people don't realize that their handy little mobile can also be switched on remotely and used as a transmitter by anyone who's got an override code. That means emergency services—and the military. The only way to make sure they can't do it is to take out the battery. No power, no signal. You don't have a cell, do you?"

"No, just the landline."

"All right. One thing we'll do here is buy one of those pay-as-you-go units and have it activated on-site. I can get around the registration codes so it won't be traceable to us. We'll use that to call Pat and Tess, then I'll switch on this one to call my parents—no point in leaving the thing dead for too long. Now, if Shaney's death was murder rather than just an accident, we know where our renegade merc was last night, so with any luck he won't know anything about your connection to the ladies. The next thing…." He took a deep breath and tried to consider where they were most vulnerable.

It was so damned easy to slip back into the mindset of being at war with the whole world. Too easy. Kevin knew it was possible that they'd already been followed, that John and his circle of friends were already in danger—but even if there was more than one enemy hunting him, it only made sense for them to be working together, not scattering their forces.

"Johnny, the next thing I'd say is let's leave the animals at the vet and see if Pat would be willing to pick them up and take them to my mother for safekeeping. I don't believe my parents are in danger. The Colonel didn't say anything about Shaney's family being attacked, and my father has a pretty impressive security system on the house. He'll see to it that the rest of the family is covered."

John nodded. "Are you sure all that's necessary?"

"No, I'm not. But—Johnny, we're dealing with people who killed two of my men rather than wait ten minutes for an all clear. They're the kind of bastards who'd shoot a stray dog, or even a stray kid, just because they had loaded guns and a moving target—so long as they wouldn't be held responsible. There's no telling who they might go after. What I probably ought to do is take you home and let the outfit set me up somewhere as bait."

"No." John closed the distance between them, moving so close Kevin could feel the warmth of his body. "You are not going off on your own to make a target of yourself."

"I said that's what I ought to do. But the problem is, if our side has found me, maybe the enemy has, too. It may already be too late."

"So you'll stay?"

"What would you do if I didn't?"

He wasn't prepared for the sheer pain that shattered Johnny's face. Then John took a deep breath and got control of himself—obviously with an effort. He turned without another word and strode off toward the store's entrance.

Kevin trotted to keep up. "Johnny!"

Another deep breath. "Look, Kev, I don't mean to put pressure on you. I really don't. But if you went off and got killed...." John stopped and turned to face Kevin, his eyes filled with tears. "I could only hope the fuckers would find me too, as soon as possible."

The words felt like a punch. "John—"

"I'm sorry. That's not rational, it's not fair, it's probably emotional blackmail, but—" Johnny threw up his hands helplessly. "You've got to understand something. When I had no choice, I made myself learn to survive—learn to keep myself together, make new connections, all the things they say make life worth living. But it's all bullshit, Kev. What makes my life worth living is having you in it. In terms of being an emotionally healthy, self-sustaining, self-actualized human being, I'm a net loss."

"Johnny—" Kevin was at a loss himself. He'd known John wouldn't want him to go, but he hadn't expected anything this heavy. "John, I'm not leaving, damn it!"

"You fucking should! I wouldn't blame you if you did—I'm not exactly the man to have at your back. I wouldn't even mind if you left me for somebody else—it would be the smartest thing you could do. I could handle that. But I can't handle your going off to get killed because you think I need—"

"*SHUT UP!*"

"—protecting," John finished, and stopped. He dragged a sleeve across his face, sniffed, and took a long, unsteady breath. "Damn. Sorry, love. PTSD crap. You have nightmares, I have these sodding waterworks."

Kevin ached to hold him, but here in a car park, he just couldn't. "Are you all right? To go in the store, I mean."

"You're not going to run off and get killed?"

"No, I won't." He hated to say it. Clearing out still felt like the one sure way he could protect Johnny, and that was more important than anything else. Well… more important than anything but keeping Johnny's trust, and apparently he couldn't do both. "I give you my word—whatever it is, we'll see it through together."

John put his hands on Kevin's shoulders, his body relaxing. "Thank you. And I'm sorry, Kev. I am not trying to be a fucking drama queen."

"I know." Kevin slapped him on the arm. "It's all right. You'd look like hell in sequins. Especially in Brighton, this time of year."

"Brighton?"

"No, I'm just throwing out a name. But we might want to put some distance between us and Portsmouth—make ourselves moving targets so our team can see who follows when we move. My instinct is to get this bastard as far from our home as we possibly can. That is—" He stopped for a moment, distracted, as a car pulled in off the road. He kept an eye on it as he finished his sentence. "That is, if this is for real. People do die in traffic accidents, and national security types do tend to see enemies around every corner. The trouble is, some of the time they're right."

"How long do you think it'll be before we find out for certain?"

That was the real question, wasn't it? Never mind the unfairness of it—the fact that they would be living in fear because someone somewhere had neglected to arrest a war criminal, and that murderous bastard had decided to hold a grudge against one of his victims who had been so inconsiderate as to survive the initial attack. The real problem was that they were potential targets and would be until the renegade merc was caught.

If he was caught. If he was even out there at all.

"Kevin?"

"I don't know, Johnny. There's just no way to know."

HOME SWEET home.

The blinds were drawn, the doors and windows locked. There had already been steel security bars in place over the two tiny windows in the cellar, but Kevin was wrapping a sheet of aluminum foil across those, and duct taping the edges along the windows. "I'm not joining the tin-hat brigade," he explained. "It's only to prevent anyone seeing in."

"There's nothing down here but an old snow shovel and some plumbing scraps."

"It keeps anyone from seeing that," Kevin said. "And actually, there's going to be a pair of motion sensors down here, front and back, on the rafters just above the windows."

"Why?"

"Shoot out the sensors with a silenced pistol, then saw the bars or blow 'em with a shaped charge. Easiest way to break in, especially from the back." Kevin said it like he'd done it, and he very likely had.

"Oh."

"Except for the doors to the garden. But those are taken care of."

When they had returned from their shopping expedition, there had been a note on the table—*No electronics. You have my word.*—with a signature John could not make out.

Kevin had given a skeptical snort when he saw it. "I'm still going to check."

The curtain across the french doors to the garden, which they'd left open, had been closed when they returned. When John had gone to draw it back, he'd been shocked to see an expandable steel gate, the sort of thing shops put up in high-crime areas, drawn across the opening and bolted to the wall studs on either side. "What the hell?"

"The key's there," Kevin said, coming up behind him, and John realized that there were two keys on a wire ring hanging on the latch knob. He reached over and turned it, and the right-hand edge of the gate sprang away from its securing bar.

"Doesn't do much for the décor," Kevin admitted, "but it's not a bad idea. The drapes should hide it well enough when it's open."

"It's—" John caught himself before he said something unforgivable.

"It's fucking ugly. I know. But it's probably all they could do on such short notice. I was wondering how we could secure this for the night—this access was one of the reasons I thought we might want to get away from here."

The disconnected kitchen phone rang again. Kevin picked it up, said, "Yes, fine," and hung up again. "Our treadmill's on the way," he said. "Would you rather meet them, or go upstairs?"

"It's up to you," John said. "Would it be embarrassing?"

"If it is, that's their tough luck." Kevin's eyes were as hard as the tone of his voice. "I will never be anything less than proud of you."

John had to kiss him for that.

Kevin held on to him so tightly he could hardly breathe. "Johnny, I'm sorry," he said when their lips parted.

"It's not you, love. I'm glad you're here with me." He caught the echo of Frodo Baggins in his words and smiled ruefully.

"'Here at the end of all things'?" Kevin quoted back.

"Oh, it's not that bad," John said, trying to sound optimistic for Kevin's sake. "In fact, think about it. Here we are, an out gay couple, with the might of the British Armed Forces protecting our honeymoon cottage. We've come a long way from poor old Turing, hounded to death when he should've been knighted for cracking Enigma."

"We're better off for now," Kevin said.

"Now is all anybody's got." He was grateful that the doorbell rang before Kevin had a chance to respond to that bit of psychological pomposity.

"Holy shit," Kevin said when he looked through the peephole.

"What?"

"I know him. It's my old troop sergeant. He can be—incredibly homophobic when he's had a few."

"Here's hoping he's sober, then," John said. "Anyway, it's two to one."

"He could kick both our arses without breaking a sweat," Kevin said sourly, then put on a neutral face and opened the door.

Chapter Twelve

THE DELIVERY man did look like a career noncom, probably somewhere in his late fifties and nearing retirement. But he didn't look like a feeble old man—more like the sort of delivery man who never had problems with thieves because he'd have a handy length of pipe in his back pocket and a willingness to use it. Built like a brick, with a grizzled buzz-cut and a smoker's miasma of tobacco clinging to his clothes, he maneuvered the trolley with its bulky package through the door as though he did it every day. "Evening, Captain."

"It's 'mister,'" Kevin said automatically. "How've you been, Sergeant? And how did you manage to draw this one?"

"We know what the fucker looks like," the man said, somehow managing to be cheerful and menacing at the same time. "Good surveillance posts, too—attic across the street and an empty flat down the alley in back."

"The man's actually been spotted?" Kevin asked.

"He's here, all right. In England, anyway. We haven't seen him here in town yet. Word came in from Customs a little while ago—that should be in these papers." He handed over a plastic invoice pouch that looked a little bulkier than the average sales packet. "Colonel needs a signed copy of something in there by tomorrow. Got a picture of our boy, too. Mug shots and fashion pose—whoever takes him out won't have to buy his own drinks for a month."

Kevin glanced at the handful of documents without opening them. John could see Kev tensing up, and could guess what was coming. "All right. Sergeant, I'd like you to meet my partner, John

Hanson. Johnny, this is Sergeant Jones, the biggest pain in the arse you can imagine, but one hell of a soldier."

John shook the hand Jones offered. "Good to meet you, Sergeant. I wish the circumstances had been better."

"They tell me you were in Bosnia," Jones said unexpectedly, without releasing John's hand. "I lost a good friend there. Peacekeepers, my arse. They should've let us shoot the bastards."

"Yes," John said. He returned the heavy grip, not sure what to expect.

Jones let go and grinned at Kevin. "Well, he's a better match for you than that silly bint in Central Comm. You surprised the hell out of everyone with this, even the Colonel."

"I'm a little surprised myself," Kevin said. "I expected you'd have a problem with it."

"Problem?" Jones chuckled at Kevin's astonishment. "Hell, no. I can see I'm not your type, but if I'd had any clue...." He grinned evilly. "Nah, it'd never've worked. Best to keep work and play separate, I always say."

Kevin didn't say anything. He didn't have to; he looked stunned.

"Always a few smart-arse youngsters who need an old soldier to keep 'em in line," Jones said with a leer. He nodded at the treadmill box, all business once more. "You need anything that's not in there, give us a call. Just pick up the kitchen phone."

"I—thanks, I will." Kevin said. "Who's in command on this one, can you tell me?"

"Colonel's running this one himself," Jones said. "It's a grudge match for all of us. Don't worry, Captain, we've got your back."

"Thanks."

"Good luck, boys." With a wink to John, the man was out the door and away.

Kevin just stood there staring at the door, bemused.

"Lots of surprises today," John said. For some reason, the Sergeant's remark about Bosnia had given him a sense of connection, and a lot of his earlier anxiety was gone, at least for the moment. But Kevin looked poleaxed.

"He's gay," Kevin said finally.

"Sounds like it. So?"

Kevin flipped the deadbolt and put the security chain across the door. "You don't understand, Johnny. Davy Jones—that's his name, God help him—there's not an insult I haven't heard him throw. I had him pegged for a gay-basher."

John moved closer and pulled Kevin close. "Sounds to me like he fancied you."

"Christ, that's all I'd need."

"Well, who wouldn't? I could hardly blame him." John let his hands roam over Kevin's back. "But he'd have to be awfully careful. After all, you might've had the best bum in the brigade, but you were his CO."

"Thank heaven for small favors."

"And don't forget, love—when Sergeant Jones joined the Army, being gay was still a crime. Who'd suspect a tough, stinking, foul-mouthed bugger like that of being a pouf?"

"Mmm." Kevin let out a deep sigh and relaxed against John's shoulder. "Poor bastard."

They stood there for a little while, just holding each other. Finally Kevin straightened. "I'm starving. What've we got that won't take long to cook? I don't want to open that Pandora's box on an empty stomach."

"I can start water for spaghetti and do something with the bagged salad."

"Sounds good."

And tonight was supposed to have been a celebration. "Kev—I know we have that bottle of champagne…."

Kevin nodded. "And a wretched mess to sort out, too. Shall we save the bubbly until this is over?"

"Yes. It isn't this place—I'm still happy to be here, but—"

"I don't feel much like celebrating either," Kevin admitted. "All I want to do right now is have something to eat, then set up the alarm system and see if we can get some sleep."

"Same here." He felt terrible for Kevin—all the day's work, and now this deadly threat instead of the peace and quiet they were hoping for. "I wish the bastard could've at least waited another week."

Kevin chuckled. "Well, you know these murdering sociopaths, Johnny—bloody inconsiderate, every one of them."

John retreated to the kitchen and set water on to boil. He thought about putting on some music as well, but music might mask the sound of someone trying to break in. Not that such a thing was very likely this early in the evening, with all the neighbors still up and about. And just what sort of music would be appropriate to the situation, and what would Kevin like? No. For now, silence would be better than the chance of irritation.

He dumped salad into two bowls, chopped some fresh carrot into the mixed greens, and brought out the half bottle of wine left over from dinner a few nights before. One glass wouldn't do more than calm them down a bit, and that might be helpful at this point.

"Salad's up," he called. Bread? Yes, they'd picked up an Italian loaf on their way to the van rental, early this morning. He sliced a few rounds, wondering at the way time seemed to shift under stress. Had this loaf really been baked just this morning? It felt like days since they'd laughed and held each other in that luxurious shower.

He heard a scraping, scuffling sound in the hall and peeked around the corner just in time to see the end of the treadmill carton sliding through the living room door. Kevin's curiosity had gotten the better of him. No surprise there. John was wondering himself. What exactly would the SAS consider appropriate equipment for two men being stalked by a professional killer?

He was also wondering just how useful he himself would be, and how much of a liability. It had been a long time since basic training, a long time since he'd fired or even held a gun, even though his marksmanship had been excellent and was probably still above average. He was reasonably fit, too—at least physically. That didn't mean he could stand up to this uncertainty.

Had he put Kevin's life in danger by insisting they stay together?

The water had come to a boil; he stirred the pasta in. Everything from the kitchen was still in boxes, but they'd brought the boxes to the appropriate rooms and—yes, there was the jar of sauce. He cheated on the home cooking by putting a saucer over the open jar and sticking the whole thing in the microwave for a minute.

He'd learned that so long as he heated in short bursts and stirred betweentimes, the jar wouldn't explode.

I'm turning into a housewife, he thought suddenly. Which was a stupid notion—he usually made dinner, but Kevin, more of an early bird, usually fixed their breakfast. They were a team. Each of them did what needed doing when a task came to hand. Wasn't that what it was all about?

"How's it going?" Kevin called from the other room.

"The salad's ready if you want it. Another few minutes on the spaghetti."

"Right."

John heard a few unidentifiable clicks, and then a sound that set his teeth on edge—the magazine of an automatic weapon chunking into place. *Well, what did you expect, water pistols?*

"Johnny, do I have time to set up the basement sensors?"

"Can you do it in under ten minutes?"

"I think so." Kevin came in through the dining room with a handful of tiny blinking devices. "Do you remember where we put my toolbox?"

"I brought that in. It's with my bike. Hall cupboard, under the stair."

"Thanks."

Kevin disappeared down the cellar stair to do what he was trained for. John told himself that his own training was not inferior, only different. There'd be no point in trying to reason with a man who was determined to kill them. There were, no doubt, some ethical men in mercenary forces. The pay was better than regular Army, and that would certainly be a factor for many. But gun-for-hire, without the safeguards of military law, was the kind of job that had a special appeal to men who could not, or would not, agree to be bound by the laws that regulated civilized warfare. Many of those men were no doubt perfectly sane. A lot of them were not.

Plates. Which box were the plates in? He rummaged a bit more and found the box of dishes tucked into a cupboard. The crumpled newspaper flew. *Civilized warfare. Jumbo shrimp. Amicable divorce.* But yes, damn it, there was a difference between an honorable soldier and a war criminal. Self-defense and defense of the helpless were ethical responses to unprovoked attack. You did your best to avoid harming civilians, you fired when fired upon. You did not take unarmed prisoners out and murder them. You didn't attack your allies for following correct procedure.

The water boiled over, and John jumped to turn down the heat. The colander. Where had they put it?

A quick search turned up nothing, and he didn't have time to hunt for it. John clapped a plate over the pot and drained away most of the water, though the towel he used as a potholder got saturated with steam. It didn't matter, he wasn't filming a cooking show. By the time Kevin emerged from the cellar, their first meal in their new home was ready.

Kevin took one look at the table and said, "You're fantastic."

"It's only spaghetti."

"It's food." Kevin went to the sink and washed the grime off his hands. "It's hot, it's here—we don't have to go out or worry about delivery...." He sat on the folding chair and leaned back with an audible sigh of relaxation. "Johnny, it's *home.* Thank you."

"I couldn't find the wine glasses," John said.

"They're in the fridge with the champagne. I put 'em in there to chill."

"Oh." Why hadn't he seen them? No matter. At least they were clean, and room-temperature red wine wouldn't damage them.

He set the glasses down; Kevin poured. They each raised a glass; their eyes met. John searched for a suitable toast and could only think of one thing. "To a quiet life."

"The sooner the better," Kevin agreed. "Damn, I nearly forgot." He got up and went to the kitchen phone. Wordlessly, he disconnected the cord from the handset. "Alone at last."

"You're joking," John said.

"No. The receiver doesn't need to be picked up for someone to listen." He smiled at John's obvious disbelief. "Didn't you know that? We used to tap into phones all the time—it's a big help if there's a situation in some place like an office building with lots of different phone lines, when you're trying to find out where hostages are being held."

"Christ." John crunched a forkful of salad. "There really is no getting away from it, is there?"

"Afraid not. Sorry."

"It's not you."

Kevin pushed his spaghetti around moodily. "Yes, it is."

"Now I say, 'Isn't!'" John had to smile. "And you say, 'Is!' and we go back and forth with it a few times, and the next thing you know there's tomato sauce all over the kitchen."

Kevin shook his head, but he was smiling too. "When you said that, I could just hear my mother saying, 'Now, children, I'll have no quarreling at the table.'"

"Are you saying I sound like your mother?"

"I'm saying I'm probably acting like a five-year-old. And I'd apologize, but that would start it all over, wouldn't it?"

"As your mother would probably say, eat your dinner." John followed his own advice. "Kev, if my choices are you with a maniac on your heels or peace and quiet without you—that's a no-brainer. We'll get through this. And as you said, there's a good chance this is all a false alarm."

Kevin glanced away, then shrugged. "That's possible."

"But now you think it's for real. Why?"

"If the Colonel's handling it himself, and has brought Jones in, and they've given me that arsenal in the other room—then they know something we don't. He wouldn't bring in that kind of firepower for a suspicious traffic accident. But let's not borrow trouble. I need to read the dossier."

They didn't get to that for another couple of hours, though, because Kevin began setting up the security system immediately after dinner. He even had John boost him up into the attic space above the upper floor so he could put a few motion sensors in up there as well. "No point putting locks on the door if they can tunnel through over our heads."

The thought of someone creeping in through the attic next door, right over their bed, shook John sufficiently that when Kevin asked him if he was willing to carry a pistol, he was ready to agree. He hoped he wouldn't have to use it, but seeing it was his lover's life that might be at stake, not to mention his own, there seemed to be little choice.

He didn't get depressed until Kevin pulled a mat of fine wire mesh from the box of equipment and began screwing its metal framework into place around the edges of their living room window, the big sunny bay window that faced onto the street. "Barrier against a firebomb or grenade," Kevin said. "This won't show much once it's stretched out, no more than a window screen, but it'll stop almost anything. The double-pane windows are already pretty tough—"

"Right," John said. "I see. You don't have to explain." He went upstairs just to get away from it for a little while and put himself to work setting up their stereo in the library, on one of the smaller bookshelves.

Some time later, slumped on the futon and listening to R. Carlos Nakai playing an American Indian flute, he heard Kevin's step in the hall. "Johnny?"

"In here."

Kevin came in and sat beside him. "Anything I can do?"

"Not really." John slid sideways so his head rested against Kevin's; his lover put an arm around him. "Better now. I think I'm—" He yawned, suddenly exhausted. "I think some of it's that I'm just tired."

"I can't imagine why," Kevin said ironically. His hand moved along John's arm, slow and comforting. "We were up at the crack of dawn, moved my things, moved your things, found out that not only is there an actual bogeyman, he's probably out there ready to pounce on us... I don't see why a few little details like that would make you tired."

"It's the cooking. Next thing you know I'll turn into a big old drag queen and slop around the house in a robe and slippers with curlers in my hair."

"Oooo, look! It's a penguin on the telly!" Kevin said in Monty Python falsetto. John cracked up, and as he was laughing helplessly, Kevin leaned over and kissed him.

John grabbed on to him. However fucked-up everything else was, *this* at least still made sense. Oh, yes.... He caught hold of

Kevin's thigh, ran his hand up the inside, and went to work on the button of Kevin's jeans.

Things would have progressed nicely from there—except that the phone in the kitchen began to ring.

"Shit!" Kevin said fervently.

"Ignore it," John mumbled against Kevin's lips. "It's not hooked up."

"Can't. The light's still on downstairs. They'll know we haven't gone to bed."

"God*damn* it—" But there was no point in arguing with the air; Kevin was already halfway down the stairs. John sat for a minute, wondering whether to just stay where he was. No, that would look like sulking, and Kevin was right. Besides, if the phone wasn't answered, the nosy, well-intentioned bastards would probably send in a squad to see if they were still alive.

When he got downstairs, Kevin was just hanging up the phone and disconnecting the receiver. "We can rule out an accident," he said. "There's more background on our merc— seems the fellow in the States who gave him his walking papers was found dead last week. At the time it didn't seem related to anything, but it jumped out when our inquiry on his previous employment came through."

"Found dead? How? Where?"

"Funny you ask. *Where* was in his own garage, under his car. He lived alone, and a neighbor reported a smell. The coroner's report said he'd been killed by impact from a large vehicle, but his car showed no signs of impact."

He let out the breath he hadn't realized he was holding. "So the body was planted."

"Amazing, Holmes. How do you do it?" Kevin neutralized the sarcasm by giving John a quick kiss. "Yes, it was obvious he'd been killed elsewhere. That's why they put it down as murder, rather than hit-and-run—and the shape and location of the impact damage made the medical examiner suggest they look for one of those damned big Hummers."

"That matches what we know of him," John said. "Overcompensation. A man who couldn't qualify as an officer in the real military might buy as many of the trappings as he could. A military-style car, expensive personal weapons, that sort of thing."

"That would fit this bastard," Kevin said. "Arrogance enough for a general, but no self-control. In a way I'm surprised he hasn't come at us head-on by now. You don't suppose my so-called resignation makes me less of a target?"

"I shouldn't try to show off—forensic psych isn't really my thing. But an educated guess—since you were the one who stood up to him in the first place, he may see you as the cause of it all. You're bound to be on the list. I'm just grateful you weren't the first target."

"I hope the bloke who made him redundant was the one who hired him in the first place."

"Yes." John gave up his last hope of seeing their lives return to normal anytime soon. "Right, then. Your sergeant said there was information in that dossier?"

"Yes. You should at least know what he looks like." Kevin retrieved the papers and spread them out on the kitchen table. "Here's our boy. Charming, isn't he?"

Not by a long shot. A set of arrest-record photos was clipped to something John automatically classified as costume drama. "Rocky Diaz," the headline declared. "A hard man is good to find." The picture was part of a half-page ad in some mercenary magazine, and from the comic-book grimace to the overloaded equipment belt, he looked like a humanoid construct out of a war-game video, not the kind of man John would have been willing to serve with. He wasn't even wearing his pseudo-Special Forces beret properly. And his eyes had the soul-dead stare of the Serbian murderers John had watched shooting down innocent civilians who happened to have had the wrong ancestors.

"'Rocky,' for God's sake," John said. "He looks like a joke. A macho asshole who's likely to get someone killed."

"Got it in one," Kevin said. "Rotten joke, though. It's a nom de farce, of course. His real name is Carl Blackwell. Diaz is his mother's maiden name, but the family's mixed-bag American."

"I'm surprised he didn't call himself Stallone."

"I'm surprised anyone hired him. He's got an assault-and-battery record going back to juvenile offenses, dishonorable discharge for striking a superior officer, and four divorces, all for violent behavior. No children, though. That's unusual—this sort of character generally leaves a string of abandoned kids by different mothers."

"Hm. Sterile, you suppose?"

"That'd be a break for the gene pool, wouldn't it?" Kevin flipped to the next page. "Drunk and disorderly, driver's license suspended for reckless driving convictions… there's a lot more. By rights he should be in prison—there's no hint he can function in normal society. Though I suppose if you want somebody who hasn't got a single human inhibition against brutality or murder, he's your boy."

"Who would be crazy enough to hire someone that volatile?"

"Corporations. Multinationals, for jobs in overseas locations where the police forces are corrupt and it's survival of the fittest." Kevin's voice was heavy with loathing. "The men in silk suits never have any contact with the actual mercenaries. They leave that to 'human resources' recruiters. Middle management, like the first man who was killed."

"Murder for hire," John said.

"Just about. And they call them 'security contractors.'" Kevin shook his head. "It's time the UN outlawed private armies in war zones. Blackwell is worse than some, but he's not all that unusual. And even if he lost his job, you can bet he kept the weapons."

"How would he bring them through Customs?"

"We don't know that he did—but he might have a cache here as well, left over from when he was in England doing bodyguard work for another branch of that company. At any rate, he's been using a car as his weapon, and anyone with a valid driver's license can rent one of those."

"Your people would've checked that, I assume?"

"Absolutely. It would be part of the basic sweep. He came in through Customs a week ago claiming to be bound for a hiking trip in Cornwall, gave them the name of a B&B where he had a reservation—"

"And never arrived."

"Of course not. And we're back to plausible situations—that happens sometimes, people change their plans, they forget how wet and cold it gets this time of year, and decide to go see a few shows in London instead. It's impossible to monitor everyone—even if the tourism industry didn't go postal at the record-keeping, the cost would be astronomical. But there's no record of him anywhere else—no credit card trail, hotel bills, car rental, bus tour—nothing. And no indication he's gone home."

John frowned at the photo. "Kev—you've done this sort of thing before, haven't you? What can we expect? How long do you think it's going to be until we can get back to some kind of normal life?"

He hated to ask, didn't want to put Kevin on the spot, but this situation was affecting him far more than he had thought it would. The grille over the doors, the mesh on the window, the knowledge that there were men outside staking them out and waiting for a killer... it was not the sort of life he'd expected to lead. Possibly not a life that he could lead for very long without having to resort to professional help.

And Kevin's face showed that he understood all that without John having to say it. "I don't know." He gathered up the papers and slid them back into the folder, leaving out what had to be the contract Jones had spoken of. "I don't know what to tell you, Johnny. I know you don't want a lie—and if I said, 'Oh, just a couple of days,' two days from now you'd know I was lying to you, and I don't want that."

"Weeks? Months?"

"God, not months—it shouldn't be months." Kevin took John's hand. "I can tell you what should be happening right now, more or less. Pictures and other info have been sent out to security at airports and borders—Customs, police, agencies that rent any sort of vehicle more aggressive than a bicycle. Blackwell may have resources, but he can't make himself invisible. Unless he's rented a boat and gone out to meet some other vessel in international waters, sooner or later someone will spot him."

John nodded. That was about what he had guessed, but Kevin's confirmation was reassuring. "That will happen sooner rather than later if he's here in Portsmouth."

"Yes, especially if he makes an attempt on this house. But—" Kevin frowned, running his free hand through his hair. "Now that I think about it, Johnny—he might not have any idea where to look for me. Since I bolted after the hearing and moved in with you, my family are the only ones who have any idea where I am. We haven't bought this place yet, so my name's not on any land title. My mail is forwarded by a woman who's been working in Intelligence since the Cold War. She's not the sort who'd let anything slip. I'm not in public records—haven't even changed the address on my car registration."

"He found your old commanding officer, though."

"Shaney? That's true. But Shaney was still on active duty, and I suppose just about anyone could have followed him home from the office or watched until he went to his local pub. When I resigned, one of the terms I insisted on was that my whereabouts be kept confidential afterwards. I didn't want to have to deal with any more damned reporters."

"So if they've kept it quiet, he could be anywhere in England. Assuming he doesn't have some sort of inside contact—"

"If he did, I'd be dead by now," Kevin said simply. "I'll have to call the Colonel tomorrow and ask him some very specific questions."

"Not tonight?"

"What difference would it make? It can wait, Johnny. They may have more information in the morning—hell, they may have caught him by morning. I just want to wash up and go to bed."

"Sounds good." As they stood, John was suddenly aware of how bone-deep tired he was. He wasn't wearing his watch, and they hadn't unpacked the kitchen clock yet, but it felt very late. "Kev, what time is it?"

"Nearly one."

"Damn."

"Yeah." He gave John a halfhearted smile. "I expected we'd be up this late tonight, but not this way." He nodded toward the telephone. "I'm going to reconnect that, just as added insurance."

"Go ahead. If you're feeling as festive as I am, there'll be nothing for them to hear."

"I still want you to wash my back." Kevin reconnected the phone. "We'll call it a night, then," he said distinctly. "I'm going to leave the light on over the sink."

They spent another few minutes checking locks and activating the various warning systems, then made their way upstairs and hit the shower. John said nothing about his misgivings, but it bothered him that he couldn't see the door from inside the shower stall. Couldn't hear anything either, with the water running.

"What's wrong?" Kevin asked.

"Nothing serious. Just worried and angry."

"Yeah, same here." Kevin handed him the sandalwood soap they'd opened that morning. "See if you can scrub some of it off me."

John lathered his hands and let himself be distracted. That wasn't a bad idea, washing off the bad vibes. It might be a primitive ritual, but when all the sophisticated analysis was said and done, it was the rituals that spoke to the soul when no amount of words could get through.

And Kevin seemed to be at his happiest when he was soaking wet. No matter what was waiting for them tomorrow, right here and now they had each other. John knelt, resting his head against one of Kev's thighs while he washed his legs, and planted a very wet kiss on Kevin's quiescent cock.

"God, that feels good," Kevin said, hands braced on John's shoulders. "Wish I wasn't so damned tired."

"I'm just as glad you are. I'm not up for anything tonight." As John stood again, his fingers ran over the irregularity of the scar on Kevin's arm. His stomach clenched, and he pulled Kevin close.

Kevin laughed. "I thought you weren't—"

"I'm not. Just want to hold you." Fear and anger might excite some men's libidos, but John was not one of them. He breathed in, made himself relax, and loosened his grip. "Sorry, love. I'm really not handling this well."

"You'll have to tell me sometime how you define 'well.'" Kevin turned his face enough to brush his lips across John's temple. "You haven't panicked. You haven't bailed. Hell, you haven't even reamed me out for dumping this mess on your doorstep, and you've every right to do that!" He took the soap out of John's hand. "Your turn."

John closed his eyes and held on to the grab bar, focusing on the strong, sure touch of Kevin's hands. Kevin knew what he was doing. His old team was out there, guarding his back. Nothing was going to get into this house; they would be all right. He did his best to imagine his fears being rinsed away and down the drain, but suspected it was his lover's attention that did the most good.

Kevin shut off the water, and the next thing John knew, he was being swathed in a warm, dry towel. "I'll tell you, Johnny," Kevin said. "I've seen the inside of a lot of safe houses, but I never saw one to match what we've got here."

"Kev," he said, feeling a little less grim. "This is a *gay* safe house. We have a stereotype to uphold."

His nice warm towel was snatched away. "Get in bed quick, and I'll pretend I didn't hear that."

"Ooh, macho man." He sprinted down the hall before Kevin could snap the towel at him, and practically dove between the clean, welcoming sheets.

As Kevin settled in beside him, John threw an arm across his lover. Even fresh from the shower, his hair faintly damp, there was something in Kevin's natural scent that stirred him. A bit of a cuddle would be nice. Or possibly more. He ran a tentative finger along the side of Kevin's jaw. "Kev, just how tired are you?"

"Hm." Kevin rolled closer. As their legs twined together, he burrowed his face into the hollow between John's throat and shoulder. "Pretty damn tired. But I might possibly be persuaded."

His breath was just warm enough to make John shiver. "Really?"

"Mm. Might take a lot of persuading."

"Oh. Well, I wouldn't want to wear you out."

"Mm. Thanks." He snuggled in closer and gave a deep sigh.

John thought Kevin was joking, until his breath caught in a faint snore. Kev was warm, naked, irresistible…, and dead to the world. John considered whether it would be worthwhile trying to wake him in some seductive way, then reflected on how long a day it had been and how sleepy he was himself, and decided that they'd both enjoy sex more if they were rested. He could tease Kev tomorrow about it, maybe challenge him to prove he wasn't already bored with domesticity.

A few years ago he wouldn't have been thinking this way or letting the chance slip by. Neither of them would. But after all that had happened, a few years ago was practically another lifetime. For now, it was enough to be warm and safe, drifting off to sleep with Kevin in his arms. Their problems could wait until morning.

Chapter Thirteen

IT WAS dark, pitch black, and the enemy was somewhere outside, waiting, just waiting for the right moment to strike. He couldn't see anything, couldn't hear worth a damn. This bunker was like a concrete box—all very well, but it wouldn't withstand a direct hit. And he didn't know what was out there, what he was facing, only that it was nearer than they thought and had no intention other than murder, and it was so close in here, every movement was like swimming in quicksand—

Someone grabbed him. They'd got in from behind! He spun, lashing out. Something caught his arm; he struggled to break free.

"Kev?"

"*No!*"

"It's okay, it's all right, love. It's all right. Calm down. Bad dream."

Panting, Kevin flailed around and found the lamp, knocking it half off the table before he got control of himself. His body went on shaking for a minute after his mind recognized that Johnny was only telling the truth. He was in bed at home. Their new home, his and John's, no pictures on the walls yet or even a headboard on the bed, but safe enough, at least for the moment. "Sorry," he said finally, angry with himself. "I thought I was finished with this shit."

"It's all right, Kev." John rummaged around on the floor—he didn't have a bedside table, something they planned to remedy eventually—and handed Kevin a plastic water bottle. "With everything that seems to be hitting the fan, it would've been a surprise if your subconscious hadn't been stirred up."

He wasn't really thirsty, but he drank some water anyway, appreciating the gesture. "Are you all right? I didn't—"

"You were tossing around. I think you got tangled up in the sheet. You didn't hit me, I'm fine. How about you?"

Kevin shook his head, looked at the clock: 3:47 a.m. Much too early to get up. "I'm all right." A look at John's neutral expression made him more honest. "No, I'm not *all right*, but there's not much I can do about it. If I were by myself, I'd just get up and read for a while, until I felt sleepy. I could do that—"

"Do you want to?"

"Leave this nice warm bed and my nice bed warmer? Not a chance." John reached out toward him, and Kevin allowed himself to be pulled down into a comforting embrace. "Johnny, I'm sorry."

"So am I, but it's nothing you've done. We'll get through it."

Kevin tried to relax, but the adrenaline was still humming through him. "The last time this happened, you said something about hypnotizing me. Were you serious?"

John hesitated a moment. "Yes, I was. But strictly speaking, it would be better for you to work with a disinterested third party."

"No." He realized that sounded harsh, and added, "Not right now, at any rate. I don't want to deal with any more health service people, and I trust you. Why wouldn't you want to do it?"

"Two reasons. Professional detachment—I haven't got any with you—plus, I'm not an expert."

"But you do know how."

"The basics. I took a course, and I've practiced on other students. I made tapes for myself that seemed to work, but—"

"That's good enough for me. As for the detachment business, so long as you don't plan to make me cluck like a chicken—"

John chuckled. "That's a myth, you know."

"No, I didn't, but let's see what you can do, at least for now. If it works, we're in good shape. If it doesn't work at all, I'm no worse off, and if it doesn't work as well as you think it should, we can decide what to do next."

John mulled that over for a minute. "All right, that's reasonable. What do you know about hypnosis? Besides the misinformation about chickens."

"Not a lot." Kevin yawned, the fatigue beginning to settle in again, but he was still too keyed up to sleep. "Just assume I'm completely ignorant. Imagine I've just walked into your office and told you I'm having trouble sleeping, but I don't want to use pills."

"All right. I'll skip the client history. We already know what's causing the problem. Sometimes people don't. The cause can be work-related, or a difficult relationship—I hope we can rule that out, at least."

Getting comfortable on John's shoulder, Kevin smiled. "No problem there. Got a great lover." He slid an arm across John's chest. "I suppose you could call this mess an old job-related annoyance."

Johnny rested his hand on Kevin's forearm, stroking the skin lightly with his thumb. "That's a good start. Now, you probably know that hypnosis is really nothing more than a state of relaxed concentration. It isn't some kind of Svengali thing. I'm not going to take control of your mind or anything like that. It's more like going to a physical trainer for coaching. You're learning how to do an exercise, a mental exercise, and I'll talk you through it at first because until you're familiar with the process, it's just easier to let me handle that part of it. I'll give you suggestions about things you can do to help yourself relax, but you're in control. You have the freedom to accept or reject anything I say if it doesn't work for you."

"Okay," Kevin said. He'd always liked Johnny's voice anyway, but he hadn't noticed before how soothing it was.

"There's nothing like what you see in films," John continued. "No flashing lights, no bells, no feeling of falling, or anything like that. It's just a feeling of relaxation. And it's another myth that stupid people are easier to hypnotize. Truth is, it's easier for someone who's intelligent and has the ability to concentrate, to focus, to learn how to go into a hypnotic state. You just start by taking a deep breath, and the reason for that is physical. Your body tenses a little when you inhale, and when you exhale, your whole body relaxes, so when you focus on your breathing, your mind becomes aware of that relaxation, and every breath lets you relax a little further. Just take a deep breath now, Kev."

Kevin did so. As he released it he felt his muscles responding and realized that Johnny was right. Nothing to it, really.

"Yeah, you see? That's all there is to it. Just breathe normally, naturally, and pay attention to the way your body relaxes when you exhale... just a little bit more relaxed with each breath. Just tell yourself, 'with every breath, deeper...' and every breath will help you continue relaxing, becoming more comfortable. You can let your eyes close now, if you like."

With another yawn, a huge one this time, Kevin did just that. It wasn't the most stimulating lecture he'd ever listened to, but the pleasant, comforting hum of Johnny's voice lulled him down into relaxation, and eventually into blessed sleep.

WHEN HE woke up, the room was full of daylight, diffused through the closed miniblinds, and Johnny was nowhere to be seen. The clock on the nightstand said it was almost ten. Kevin stretched luxuriously. He didn't remember the rest of the hypnosis session, but either John had done it and it had worked a treat, or he simply gave the most boring, sleep-inducing lecture known to man. Kevin hoped for the former—and he also hoped John's future clients would be given slightly less consideration than he had been. He wasn't going to stand for having his lover hypnotize his clients and snuggling up with them stark naked.

Feeling unexpectedly optimistic, Kevin rummaged in his suitcase for fresh underwear, then had a shave and headed downstairs. He found an absurdly domestic scene—John, in his habitual sweatpants, washing up the dishes they'd left from the night before, the teakettle just coming to a boil on the cooker. "Sorry I fell asleep before you could hypnotize me," Kevin called above the sound of running water.

"You didn't," John said over his shoulder.

"I must have, Johnny. I don't remember a word you said beyond telling me to relax when I exhale." Kevin rescued the screaming kettle and poured water over the tea already waiting in the pot. "Slept well, though." He carried the pot to the table, then went over to give his industrious lover a kiss on the back of the neck. "What would you like for breakfast?"

"You went under, love." John turned around, laughing, and pointed. "Look at your pants."

"What—?" Kevin glanced down and was horrified to find himself wearing the nether garment that John had, in a fit of whimsy, bought for him the day they'd signed the lease. Skintight briefs in screaming fluorescent orange were not his style at all, still less when they had *WEAPON OF MASS SEDUCTION* blazoned across the front. He had, of course, refused to wear the damned things. "Johnny, you said no Svengali tricks!"

"Kev, I asked if you'd be willing to put those on, just this once, to prove you were really hypnotized, and you said yes."

"Hypnotized? I must've been insane!"

Johnny was wiping his hands dry on a towel, his grin shifting from warm to wicked. "I promised I'd take them off you. Slowly."

"Right now?"

"Why not?" He tossed the towel on the counter and put his arms around Kevin, hooking his thumbs in the waistband and sliding them down. "We've done the bedroom and bath so far... why not the kitchen?" His hands were hot from the dishwater. Kevin shivered at the contrast to the cooler air in the room.

He glanced at the phone as Johnny began nuzzling his neck, saw that John had prudently rendered it incommunicado. "Too bad we don't have a decent table."

"Who needs a table?" Johnny pulled him closer and turned Kevin around so that he was braced against the sink front. "You realize it's been more than twenty-four hours?"

The way he said it made hours sound like weeks, and Kevin felt the same way. "Let's fix that, then." He grabbed Johnny's face and kissed him, distracted from the hard edge of the counter behind him by the hot, hard pressure of the body holding him against it.

Kevin pulled at John's sweatpants, but John caught his hands.

"No, I said I'd take *your* pants off." John kissed him again, lingeringly, then turned his attention elsewhere.

Kevin shivered as Johnny kissed down his throat and licked along his collarbone, blowing cool air over wet skin at the same time he ran his thumbs over Kevin's nipples.

By the time Johnny slid slowly to his knees, Kevin had both hands buried in his hair. "You can take 'em off now," he said hopefully.

"Not yet." John eased the waistband a little lower, rubbing his face against the fabric and Kevin's cock, tracing the length of it with his lips as it responded to the attention.

"Johnny, damn it—" He might just have been able to control himself if it had only been that one point of contact, but Johnny's hands were busy too, running up the back of his thighs, working their way under the briefs from beneath. He pulled the waistband down just far enough for Kevin's cock to slip free; the slight pressure of the elastic against his balls created a weirdly erotic sensation. But he couldn't pay much attention to that either because John's hands were pinning his thighs just as he took the sensitive tip of Kevin's cock into his mouth.

A good thing he was holding on. Kevin bucked involuntarily and nearly toppled even with the support. He dug his fingers into John's shoulders and simply held on as the waves of pleasure mounted, built toward a peak—

And the phone rang.

Johnny ignored it.

Past the point of no return, Kevin felt his body climax even as a part of his brain counted the telephone rings. Five... six... seven....

It stopped, and John looked up at Kevin. He caught hold of the counter, pulled himself to his feet, and dropped a kiss on Kevin's damp forehead just as the phone began to ring again. "I'll get it." He connected the receiver and lifted it. "Hello?"

Kevin started to take a step forward, realized the damn briefs were now down around his knees, and pulled them back up.

"No," John was saying. "It's not convenient at all. The phone's in the kitchen, and it's difficult to hear when the shower's running. Is this an emergency?" He listened to whatever the other party said, and responded, "All right, then. Any harm if he calls you back in about twenty minutes? Thank you." He didn't bother to hang the receiver back up, just disconnected it and dropped it on the table. He splashed his face at the sink and toweled dry. "Damned busybodies."

"I could've got that," Kevin said.

"Not unless you wanted Sergeant Jones to know what you sound like when you're shagged out. I don't think that comes under 'need to know' for him."

"I don't—"

"Yes, you do. You sound all warm and fuzzy, like you just had the best kitchen sex of your life. I don't want him getting any hotter for you than he already is."

Somewhat recovered, Kevin checked in the cupboard and found to his surprise that their usual mugs were in there. He filled them with tea and set them on the table. "I didn't realize you had a jealous streak."

John nodded thanks and sat down. "I'm not jealous of random men, love. But a whole damned squad? They seem to think we're sitting here desperate and dateless, waiting for them to call. At any rate, it isn't an emergency. Jones says they have some new information."

"They could've told you that just as well."

"Yeah, that's what I thought." Johnny sipped at his tea. "Must be for your ears only."

"Twenty minutes," Kevin said. "Want to go back to bed for a little while?"

John shook his head. "Thanks, no. Not after that mood-breaker."

He looked understandably disgruntled, and Kevin felt a pang of guilt. "Guess I should've asked about sex last night, instead of hypnosis."

"Oh, I'll get over my sulk soon enough. At least I got to see you in those pants, and you're right—that's not your color. Will cold cereal do?"

"Fine."

They ate quickly, wanting to get the meal over with before Kevin had to make that phone call. Johnny finished first, and as he rinsed out his bowl, he said, "Kev, it's not that I don't appreciate your team being out there, but every time that phone rings, my whole body goes on red alert—and I can't go out and run or ride my bike to burn off the adrenaline."

"And their timing couldn't be worse," Kevin agreed. "But we have to maintain communication—" He caught himself. It wasn't his mission anymore, or his team. *His* team was right here at the table, stuck in a wretched situation through no fault of his own. "What do you need, Johnny? What do you want me to do?"

John sighed as he dropped back into his chair. "If there's a crisis, of course they have to call immediately. I realize that. And they waited till ten in the morning, when they could've called hours earlier. I can't complain about that. It's the not knowing that gets to me—thinking every call might be an emergency. Do you suppose they'd be willing to set up some sort of schedule, maybe check in at even-numbered hours?"

Kevin realized he should have thought of that. "A schedule would be good. That would give us a time for the first call of the day— I could phone in at a set time in the morning, whatever o'clock and all's well, and if all's well at their end, we could just go back to bed."

"That should help."

"At least it wasn't as bad as the time my mother called when we were otherwise occupied."

"But she left a message. This stupid thing—" Johnny spun the disconnected receiver on the table. "I damn near told them the truth," he said, and Kevin suddenly realized there was real anger under his reasonable demeanor. "I just couldn't think of a way to describe what we were doing that wouldn't embarrass you." He picked up his mug.

"You could've said you're too polite to talk with your mouth full," Kevin suggested. As the tea splattered across him, he realized he should've waited until his partner had swallowed.

"Sorry—" Johnny finally managed. He tried to compose his expression, but the corners of his mouth kept turning up. "I am. Really."

"That's okay, we can take a shower when I'm finished here." Kevin snagged the dish towel and mopped himself and the table.

"I already showered." Johnny gave him an apologetic smile and a kiss. "I want to start unpacking things in the bedroom, love. If the coast is clear, come on up—I'm not playing hard to get."

"I'll hold you to that," Kevin promised. He picked up the phone, which he was beginning to hate. This was twice now that he'd let Johnny down, and that was twice more than he'd ever done or meant to do. Ah well. Check in, find out if there was anything they needed to do, then go coax Johnny out of those baggy sweats. If he was sorting out the bedroom, that bottle of massage oil would be somewhere to hand, and it shouldn't be too difficult to distract him. Maybe there'd even be good news, and they could go out to dinner to celebrate.

But the news was minimal. Blackwell had used a credit card to buy a meal in London the night he'd arrived at Heathrow. That was the kind of information that would be part of a mosaic, a valuable part—if there were any other data to put with it. There wasn't. Kevin hung up, disgusted, and went upstairs.

Chapter Fourteen

"ANY NEWS?"

"Nothing."

They had been living this way for three days. They had unpacked everything, put up the bookshelves in the library, and rearranged the living room twice. Their computers—John's older desktop model, Kevin's laptop—had been established in the nook off the library. If they hadn't been trapped in the house, the place would have seemed roomy and comfortable. As it was, nothing seemed more desirable than a walk down the street—not only was it a waste of expensive, highly trained manpower to have milk delivered by a disguised special-ops trooper, but both he and Johnny were in serious need of fresh air and exercise.

On the bright side, Kevin had been sleeping soundly, and John had assured him that he had left no more posthypnotic suggestions about underwear. But they were both getting restless, and after lunch on the third day, John took serious exception to the kitchen wallpaper, declaring that it had to go or he would.

He had never quoted Oscar Wilde before. Kevin took that as a sign that Johnny was really feeling the strain, and agreed immediately that it was well past time. They soaked the stuff down with vinegar solution and scraped the walls down to a creamy yellow that had been the previous color. Apart from the whole house smelling like a jar of pickles, Kevin had to admit that the change was for the better.

But they had finished that project a couple of hours ago, and John was back to roaming through the house looking for something to do, while Kevin sat on the sofa, occupied with a pad of graph paper.

"Would you like to watch *The Lord of the Rings*?" Kevin offered. "The extended version?"

Johnny stopped on his migration between kitchen and front window. "Is it that bad, then? I'm sorry."

"No—we've talked about a movie marathon. Why not now?"

John dropped down beside him. "Kev, this isn't working."

"Would you rather send the Army out for a gallon of paint for the kitchen?"

"No. And don't start snogging me either—I'm—" Kevin's notebook caught his attention. "What are you working on?"

"Oh, this. I'm probably planning too far ahead, but—" He showed John the sketches he'd made. "When I went up in the attic, it struck me that we could recover some of the living space that was lost when they put in the spa bath. I just wanted to rough out a couple of ideas."

"The roof pitch seems really steep," John objected. "Wouldn't the space be too narrow?"

"It is steep, but it's steep and high—there's more room up there than you'd expect. The center peak is at least a meter above my reach. If we just insulated between the rafters and put the ceiling at a comfortable level—maybe have pot lights installed—the usable space would be eight or ten feet wide and the full length of the house."

Intrigued, John moved closer, his arm stretching along the back of the sofa. "Where would we put the stairway? No room for that, it would come up where the roof goes down."

"The easiest thing would be a spiral staircase. Right here, just inside what's now our bedroom door. We'd have to shift the door, over here"—he pointed—"and take out the closet, but that would give us room for separate offices, which we're going to need eventually. If we got wildly ambitious, we could even make the top floor a master suite."

"But we can't start in on that until we buy the place, can we? *If* we buy the place."

"Well, no, not yet." Kevin leaned against John's warmth, slightly amused at his own domesticity. After all the times he'd complained about being roped into his father's property-improvement projects, he was finding surprising enjoyment in his own nest-building. Due to having someone to nest with, no doubt. "But I expect we will want to stay—particularly if we want to avoid losing our deposit because we vandalized the kitchen wallpaper."

"That wasn't vandalism. That was an act of kindness."

"I agree, Johnny. And once it dries, the kitchen will look better and roomier with some yellow paint."

"White."

"Cream?"

"Off-white?"

"Let's get color cards and negotiate." Kevin could have kicked himself as soon as he said it for putting Johnny back on track. All his careful maneuvering, shot to pieces.

John saw his chagrin and laughed ruefully. "I'm not asking Sergeant Jones to go pick up paint chips for us. That's beyond daft." He let his arm slide down Kevin's shoulder and leaned in to kiss him. "And you get full marks for diversionary tactics, but we really need to decide what we're going to do about this situation."

Kevin enjoyed the kiss without trying to turn it into something more. He wasn't about to insult John by pretending he didn't know what he was talking about. "What do you have in mind?"

"I'm not sure, Kev. But—even putting off starting my house-officer post, which I can't do for much longer—I can't keep living like this."

"What's the deadline on the job?"

"Either I start January seventh, or I have to apply for an extension. And if I do that, I have to apply by the end of next week. I'd rather not delay the job if I can help it."

"We should be through with this by then."

"We hope we'll be done with it," John said. "No reason to believe we will—not from what we've seen so far."

"True. You could go to and from your job with a bodyguard."

John snorted. "God, wouldn't that be a sight. But I suppose they'd fit right in—it's a veterans' assistance center."

"So you don't really need to ask for an extension."

"No. But I'll be ready to check in myself, by then." He ruffled Kevin's hair and rose, resuming his restless pacing. "Kev, if this isn't resolved, and soon, I'm going to be in trouble."

"Can't you use your hypnosis?"

"Been there, doing that." His smile was forced. "I'm not listening to music while you watch the news, love. You don't want to know what I'd be like without those tapes."

The pain in his eyes made Kevin's stomach twist. "And I can't distract you with wild sexual excess?" he said lightly.

"You do. Any time we're in the same room, I can feel you mentally undressing me. It's incredibly distracting." John seemed uncertain whether he wanted to move or sit; he swooped down onto the sofa again and lay back against the end cushion with his legs across Kevin's lap. "But we can't shag every minute, and I can't shut off my mind."

Kevin rubbed his lover's knee, hoping it was a comforting gesture rather than an annoyance. "At the risk of sounding like a broken record, what would—"

"I'm not sure what I have in mind. But from what you've told me—from what they've told you—it seems as though you did an excessively professional vanishing act, and Blackwell—if he's out there—is just as good at staying invisible. How long do we sit here and wait until he launches a rocket through the upstairs window? Or until the government gets tired of paying our minders and we wind up facing the bastard on our own?"

Kevin shook his head. "I don't think they'll back off unless they know for certain he's gone somewhere else. It seems like forever to us, Johnny, but three days isn't all that long for this kind of job—and he's killed one of their own. There's a murder warrant out on him now, both here and in the States. I don't think he can call on his former employers to pull him out this time."

"I understand that." John sat up, frowning at the window, with its drawn curtains. "It's just—Kev, do you realize what it was that pushed me over the edge, that finally made me crack?"

Kevin didn't know how to answer that. He could guess, but he couldn't know.

"It was the waiting—partly that. But the worst of it was just what you'd predicted—the helplessness. Knowing *something* was going to happen, and no matter what it was, I wouldn't be able to do a damned thing about it. So what I'd like to do now is—anything. Just about anything that can get this situation moving." He jumped up again, as though his own stillness was more than he could stand. "But at the same time, I don't want you in danger." He met Kevin's eyes. "Your turn, now—what do you want to do? What would you do, if I weren't here?"

"Those are two different questions," Kevin said.

"I know. Sorry."

"What I want to do is go out and hunt him down, see how he likes it to be in my territory with a warrant out on him. I want to kick his balls so far up they come out his ears. But that's just wishful thinking until he shows up. Given that the troop owes me one, I would probably just take a few more days off and let them do the tedious work." He grinned apologetically. "Sorry. You've had a quieter life than I have, these past few years. Or maybe I have a higher tolerance for comfortable boredom."

"Lazy sod," John said affectionately.

"I am." An idea struck him, something so obvious he could have kicked his own arse for not thinking of it sooner. "But you know what we should do for now? Have Jones pick up the treadmill box as though we're exchanging it, and bring you a real one—or a stationary bike, or an elliptical machine. Maybe two different machines, so we can both work out at the same time and cross-train. We could put them in the cellar, make an exercise room down there, set up a TV and video. And put in a couple of full-spectrum lights, as well—that's supposed to be useful against depression, isn't it? It wouldn't be as good as getting outdoors, but it would be something."

"That would help, I think," Johnny said. "But it's not a solution, is it?"

"No. And you're right, even on my own, I would get restless eventually. It wouldn't be much longer before I'd suggest a little more visibility—doing the usual sort of thing, shopping, dinner out, find myself a local. I'd expect a few days of quiet, because if he's out there stalking, he'd most likely wait for me to let my guard down. Once I'd established a pattern, I'd expect some kind of attack within a week."

John's jaw tightened. "And what are they expecting—your former colleagues?"

"The same as I am—they're hoping the sodding bastard will get stopped for a traffic offense, picked up by routine police work. Or, next best, that he'll show his face here in town and they'll be able to take him quietly. But if not—the next practical step would be the same."

"Start making a target of yourself."

"Yes."

John closed his eyes, his graceful hands curling into fists.

"It isn't the only way, Johnny. But it would be faster—and I don't want to risk him giving us the slip. Three days has been bad enough. Can you imagine what it would be like if he were to just disappear? I don't want to spend the rest of our lives looking over our shoulders, jumping every time we hear someone rev an engine."

"God *damn* it."

Kevin agreed. "I wish I'd known about Blackwell before I came back. I should have cleaned up old business before I came dragging home to you with that on my tail."

"If anyone had known about him, they'd have hauled *his* arse into your hearing," John said angrily. "It should have been him on trial in the first place, not you."

"Yeah, if." Talking it over had irritated Kevin out of the patience he'd worked so hard to achieve. He *was* tired of waiting, tired of letting other people make the decisions. But putting Johnny at risk wasn't the option he'd choose. "I think it would be better to take the initiative. And I know you said you wouldn't go to a safe house, but—"

"I'm not going to run and hide, love. I may not have commando training, but I was a better marksman than you, remember?"

"I remember." And it surprised him to realize it, but of all the men he'd served with, Jones included, there was no one he would trust with his life more than the man beside him. *An army of lovers cannot fail. I hope.* "I'll ask if there's a target range somewhere at the old Naval Academy. We should both get in some practice with the weapons they issued us."

"Fine with me." There was a new tone in Johnny's voice, an edge of resolution. Their eyes met as John laced his fingers through Kevin's. "We're not letting that bastard derail our honeymoon. As far as I'm concerned, what we've got is till death do us part."

Chapter Fifteen

RESOLUTION OR not, they both felt the winter's bite when they left the house the following evening. A sleeting rain was blowing fine as needles in the icy wind.

"It was a dark and stormy night," Johnny said under his breath.

"I haven't written a word yet," Kevin countered. "And if you think I'm going to start with Snoopy—"

"Actually, it was Bulwer-Lytton, but you can go for dull if you like. 'The sun had gone down hours earlier, and the weather was inclement.' That should cure anyone's insomnia."

It was a stupid thing to quibble over, but it was a distraction—probably why Johnny had started the foolishness. Kevin didn't want to talk about what they were doing, making targets of themselves. His nerves were stretched tight by how exposed they were on the quiet street, and he knew John must be in much the same state.

The walk to the pub should take no more than ten minutes. It wasn't John's local, just the closest to where they now lived. And it wasn't as though they were unprotected, either. They were being watched every step of the way by soldiers stationed in buildings and parked cars. The body armor hidden under their bulky sweaters and jackets gave an extra measure of protection. But none of it was enough to provide peace of mind.

"Think we'll see him tonight?" John asked quietly.

"It's possible. Not likely."

"I almost wish he'd try. Be nice to have it over."

"I wouldn't object." But Kevin didn't want Blackwell to make an attempt tonight, not really. Body armor would be no use at all against the crushing force of a vehicle, and the narrow streets and alleys meant it might not be possible for them to avoid such an attack—or for Jones and his men to stop it.

They stopped at the corner. "Cross or turn?" John asked.

"Turn," Kevin said. The cars parked on the near side formed a convenient barricade, and he knew that one member of the team had strolled down the block just minutes ahead of them to make certain those cars were empty. Their footsteps set a rhythmic counterpoint to the patter of rain. Two more blocks straight ahead, then across the street to the pub on the corner.

A car's engine growled as they cleared the last building before the cross street at the end of the first block. Kevin caught John's sleeve to keep him in the shelter of the building and scanned the storefronts, spotted a doorway a few yards back that they could duck into—

But the dark sedan that pulled up to the corner and paused before making its turn was just a car, the driver an older gent who never even glanced at the two tense young men standing a few feet back from the curb. The taillights receded slowly until they disappeared around a bend in the road.

"That was fun," Johnny said, his voice tight.

"Fresh air and exercise." Kevin took a deep breath and stepped out again. The streets were very quiet—no one with any sense would be out in this weather—and they made it the rest of the way to the pub without encountering another soul.

It was quiet inside, too. Kevin felt himself relax a bit as they stepped into the warmth. The aroma of something delicious wafted around them on the indoor warmth. After the days of isolation, it was almost strange to be out among people, but you couldn't honestly call this a crowd. Half a dozen patrons occupied tables near the front windows and a twentysomething couple sat at the bar, the girl looking at her watch as her boyfriend talked to someone on a mobile phone, ignoring her. Kevin saw one of their minders down at the far end of the bar, sitting at an angle that let him watch the entire place. Their eyes met, then moved on; neither acknowledged the other.

Kevin took a table near the back, beside the fireplace. He could see the entrance from there, as well as the fire exit beside the loo. There should be a covert team stationed out in the alley, just in case. A pity they weren't just out for an evening; the pub was a relaxed, comfortable place, with its old oak wainscoting and dark green walls. A gas log flickering against the opposite wall completed the picture of a cozy retreat.

"It'll be nice to have a meal we didn't fix ourselves, and no washing-up after," Johnny said, looking over the menu. "Hmm. This may take a little thought."

"You've never been here?"

"No, never came down this way. Looks like I should have—it's going to be a tough choice. They've got a lot of veggie meals, Kev."

"So I see." There really was quite a selection, Italian and Indian, as well as the more usual fare. "Hm. Mushroom-walnut stroganoff. That sounds good."

"I think I'll have the turkey curry. Cross-cultural." In response to Kevin's puzzled frown, John explained, "American Indian bird, Asian Indian sauce. Oh, and they've got winter ale. Would you like a pint?"

"Sure." While John went to get their drinks, Kevin checked his mobile phone for text messages. If they appeared to be in immediate danger, Jones would call; otherwise, whoever was in charge of communications would send them an update or all clear every ten minutes. There were two all clears queued up, and no voice mail.

Kevin had a hunch the Colonel had been waiting for them to volunteer for this sort of thing. He had accepted their offer of help without hesitation, immediately doubled the number of men assigned to the mission, and provided a few suggestions as to how and where they might appear in public. He also recommended that when they were away from home, a team of soldiers would be posted in the house, in hopes of catching Blackwell if he should attempt to set up an ambush.

They'd agreed to all of it. Anything that shortened this center-stage, looking-over-the-shoulder kind of life was worth putting up with, at least for a little while.

"Any messages from your secret admirer?" John asked, returning with two pints.

"All quiet on the Portsmouth front," Kevin said. "It's what we could expect, at this stage."

"I gave them our order, without starters," John said. "Hope you haven't changed your mind."

"No, that's fine. We'll be served quicker this way, and I'd rather not stay out too long."

"Same here. It's funny, I thought I'd enjoy an evening out, but...." John shrugged. "I suppose it's the Teflon underwear— crimps one's style."

"No doubt someone, somewhere has a fetish for the stuff," Kevin said. "Doesn't do much for me."

"Oh, so you want to take it off before we go to bed?" Johnny feigned a look of mild disappointment. "I thought all you Special Forces boys had surprising kinks."

"That's probably why I washed out. Too damned normal." What was surprising, though not at all kinky, was that he felt not the slightest twinge when he said it. "I'd rather be with you than with them, anyway."

Their food arrived. "That was quick," John said as the waiter began transferring the dishes from tray to table.

"You picked two of our top favorites. There's always curry on, and the cook just finished a batch of the stroganoff. Enjoy!"

As Kevin had guessed, the stroganoff was what had smelled so enticing when they first walked in, and the taste was even better.

"Looks like hobbit food," John said. "Lots of mushrooms."

"It's excellent. How's yours?"

"Tastes like chicken." He grinned at the cliché. "Actually, it tastes like curry, but it's good, too. Want a bite?"

They traded samples and decided Kevin's entrée was more interesting. "But you know," John said, "in our grandparents' day, it would've been the other way around. We have so much Eastern food now that we take it for granted."

"I wonder if Queen Victoria ever imagined the way the whole British Empire would wind up in our restaurants," Kevin mused.

"I expect the old girl's spinning in her grave," John said. "She'd have taken a dim view of us, for certain."

Kevin raised his glass. "Here's to a long and happy rotation for Her Majesty."

Sitting there chatting with John, he actually managed, for a little while, to forget about the threat that hung over them. But in too short a time, they were pulling on their jackets, paying their check, and preparing to go back out into the cold to make targets of themselves.

The entryway had a tiny vestibule space, an airlock between the cold outside and warmth within. Kevin closed his eyes as he stepped into it, counting off thirty seconds.

"What's wrong?" John asked.

"In half a minute, I'll have some of my night vision back. Three minutes would give more, but we don't want to be too conspicuous."

"Good grief."

"I know—sorry, I don't mean to be a nuisance." He shouldered the door open into sleet and pulled his watch cap from his pocket.

"You aren't," John said, winding his muffler up to his ears. "I didn't realize how much was going on in your head—all the cloak-and-dagger details."

"I just want to be certain I see Blackwell before he sees us." The street had been checked minutes before they left the pub, but Kevin crossed so they'd be walking back on the opposite side. He found himself compulsively peeking into parked cars, just in case.

John snorted. "To hell with that—I want Sergeant Jones to see him before he sees us."

"I like the way you think." One block covered, no cars. "Johnny, I probably don't need to say this, and I don't want you to take it the wrong way—"

"Bloody hell. How bad is it? Did I do something stupid?"

"No! No, I was just thinking ahead. If anything should happen, the worst thing you could do is to try to throw yourself on top of me or fling yourself into harm's way." He winced at John's dead silence. "I'm sorry, I put that badly. It's no reflection on your ability, Johnny—I was just thinking about what I would do to protect you, and realized you'd probably have the same impulse. I don't want us to trip each other up trying to save each other. We'll both be safer if each of us just gets himself out of the way."

"I understand," John said at last.

"Sorry—"

"No, you're right. We have to treat this as a potential combat situation. Each of us has to trust the other to do his job." The corner was approaching. "Cross or turn?"

"Turn. Of course, if you see something and it's obvious I don't—" Kevin glanced toward John for a moment, and the corner of his eye caught a door fly open just behind them, a man's figure come charging out.

Completely forgetting what he'd just said, he reacted instinctively. He elbowed John out of the way and caught the stranger's outstretched arm, dropping his own weight to throw the intruder off-balance, spinning him around and then pinning him against the brick shopfront with an arm around his throat. He heard a shrill whistle, heard footsteps running toward them, and looked over to Johnny—who was staring open-mouthed as a young woman, framed in the doorway, began screaming her head off.

Oh, shit. As Jones and three men from his squad converged, Kevin heard John hushing the woman, explaining that there had been a stakeout, they had accidentally walked into a surveillance situation, he was very sorry, was she all right?

Kevin shifted his weight so the man he'd pinned could get his balance back. He hadn't been entirely mistaken—the poor bastard did bear a strong superficial resemblance to Carl Blackwell, but he was several years younger and apparently scared speechless.

"I'm terribly sorry," he said to the civilians. "Bodyguard work, you know."

They didn't know, of course, but they both nodded numbly.

"Best get our consultant away from the scene, sir," Jones said, a little too loudly. "We'll sort this out."

Damn, damn, damn. Kevin's face was burning as he and Johnny walked hurriedly away. A fine thing for him to lecture John, then in the same breath, make such a stupid mistake.

"I didn't see him," John said after they'd crossed the street. "Didn't see a thing. If that had been Blackwell, you'd have saved both our lives."

"But it wasn't him."

"It could have been. Easily. And if it had been, I'd have been very glad you were so quick. Kev, I've never seen anyone move like that, outside a martial-arts film."

"You don't watch those."

"I've seen a couple. They looked fake. This looked real."

"It was real. Except it wasn't a real attack. Damn it to hell!" He wished Johnny would stop trying to make him feel better. He had been a damned fool, and nothing could fix that.

"You're my action hero, Kev." This in an awestruck tone better suited to a teenage girl than a military veteran.

It had the desired effect, though—Kevin had to laugh. "Oh, please." As they approached their home, his mobile phone rang. The readout said it was the Colonel. That was all he needed. "Yes, hello."

"Kendrick. Your in-house team left through the rear entrance. They locked the security gate and set the rear outdoor motion sensors."

"Right. Thank you." That was something, anyway—he wouldn't have to face any more of his former teammates, at least not this evening.

"By the way, nice recovery," the Colonel said.

"What?" John had unlocked the door; Kevin followed him inside.

"That unexpected civilian. Jones nearly put a bullet into him, but you were in the way. You saved us a lot of grief—and that young idiot's life."

"It was all I had time for—"

"Lucky for all of us. I've got you both scheduled for target practice tomorrow afternoon. We'll call at ten with the specifics. Good night."

"Good night, sir." Somewhat bemused, he put the phone back in its holster.

"What was that last about?" Johnny asked. "Not a bad night's work, then," he said when Kevin finished explaining. He put his coat away in the closet and handed out a coat hanger.

"It wasn't anything I did purposely," Kevin said.

"You used enough force to neutralize what you saw as a threat, love. And not one bit more force than necessary. I'd rank that well above blowing holes in some kid who happened to pop out the wrong door at the wrong time." John hung Kevin's coat alongside his own. "It's a little past ten. Want to make an early night of it?"

"You go on up. I want to check the system."

"Tub?"

Suddenly weary, he couldn't decide between the luxury of feeling warm all over and the simple relief of crawling between the sheets and curling up in Johnny's arms. "Doesn't matter."

"I'll start it, then. If you don't want a soak, I'll just peel you out of your gear and give you a wash." Without warning, John caught Kevin's face in his hands. "You were amazing," he said. "Don't put yourself down because you aren't omniscient." Kevin was too tired to argue, and not fool enough to reject the warm kiss that brought him back down to earth. Then, with a smile, Johnny went bounding up the stairs.

Kevin shook his head and took care of securing the house. How was a man supposed to go on a guilt trip with someone like John interrupting his self-pity party? The only thing for it was to go soak in the tub with his gorgeous, considerate lover—and try not to think about how very close he had come to breaking that innocent bystander's neck.

Chapter Sixteen

A STRAY shaft of sunlight found its way under one slat of the miniblinds in the bedroom and landed with gentle persistence on John's left eyelid. At first he slept on, but after a moment, the brightness had its effect; he blinked, shifted his head slightly, and realized he hadn't adjusted the blinds last night when he'd taken a last look out at the back garden.

Kevin slept soundly beside him, the side of his face mashed against John's shoulder. Small wonder he was so zonked—he'd been friskier the night before than he had been since this Blackwell mess started, certainly more amorous than the night before that— Tuesday night—after that fiasco on their walk home. Kevin had been badly shaken by his own overreaction, and the romantic spa tub evening John had hoped for wound up in a perfunctory wash followed by a long, restless night.

Yesterday they had gone out again, playing tourist at the Naval Museum, and seen a bit more than the average sightseer was privy to. They were the only audience for the 2:00 p.m. Battle of Trafalgar presentation, and just as the taped cannon started booming in the gun deck diorama, a doorway opened at one end of the exhibition chamber—an event not on the printed schedule. From within, a polite young Naval officer invited them behind the scenes and through a series of tunnels that took them somewhere under the old Naval Academy to a firing range where John learned that the automatic he'd been issued was accurate, and so was his aim.

It was even better to discover that he had no residual issues about firing the gun. He didn't like the noise—never had—but just like riding a bicycle, the body memory was easy to access, and his hand-eye coordination was as good as it had ever been.

He also learned something that surprised him at first—though it made perfect sense. Kevin's additional field experience had brought his skill up to and equal with John's. In fact, given that Kev had actually been in life-or-death combat situations, he had experience under fire that John lacked. But instead of feeling competitive, as he might have years ago, John was pleased by the way the outcome of their practice seemed to boost Kevin's self-confidence.

And he wasn't just pleased in some abstract, self-sacrificing way. Kevin had been more his old self last night, romantic and playful. He'd hinted that the massage he'd refused the night before would be more than welcome, and John had the pleasure of working the tension out of every inch of his lover's strong, sensual body. And then Kev had appropriated the oil and returned the favor with dividends, and, of course, things went considerably beyond a relaxing rubdown. They played, and slept, and played some more, finally stopping for a late supper and the beddy-bye call to their minders.

Then it was back to bed—but not to sleep. John didn't know when they'd finally dropped off, but he'd bet any money Kevin had slept right on through after that, free of the death-dreams and nightmare fears. Sex might not be the answer to everything, but it certainly helped. If only they could stay here like this for a few days—close themselves away from the outside world, put it all in suspended animation, have a little time to pull themselves back together.

John hoped that the crisis, when it came, would be resolved thoroughly enough to allow Kevin to relax the tight control he had imposed on himself. It was really no surprise that Kevin had developed that trait—his father was pretty typical of the career military man, expecting his children, and especially his sons, to be good little soldiers and follow orders.

Kevin was smart; he had learned to adapt to that heavily structured life, but he was also introspective enough to realize that being gay set him outside his father's definition of a real man. He had done his best to keep what was useful and discard the rest.

Still…. Kevin might have consciously severed his father's domineering authority after that interview before the hearing, but the habits of a lifetime didn't change so easily.

Selfishly, John was grateful for Kevin's self-control. He'd gone out once or twice with fools who behaved as though passion and recklessness were synonymous; he appreciated having a partner who was willing to deal with his own feelings. But at the same time, he didn't want to see Kevin suppress everything until it blew out in nightmares—and while there were hypnotic suggestions he could make to counter that, he had his own integrity to consider. He couldn't let himself slip into the seductive trap of manipulating Kevin "for his own good." That would be disastrous for them and their relationship.

Moving very slowly so as not to wake his lover, he shifted so he had an arm around Kev, who mumbled something and burrowed closer. It was going on 9:00 a.m., and they'd have to be up and about by ten for the morning's first phone call.

The alarm would go off in half an hour, anyway. They had an excursion planned for this afternoon, a trip to buy paint—another perfectly ordinary errand. Since neither of them was working a regular job at the moment, they wouldn't have the usual home-to-work routine that a stalker might be able to learn. But in a new home, even small projects like painting a kitchen could require frequent excursions.

And the store's being a little way out of town would be better for their purposes. The holiday crowds were already showing up in Portsmouth for Christmas events, and it would be too easy for their quarry to hide in a throng—as well as more dangerous to the civilians if Blackwell used them for cover. Better for everyone if they established a pattern that took them out onto open roads. If Blackwell was bent on using an SUV as a weapon, they'd be safer inside another vehicle, even Kevin's little car.

But they didn't have to face that for another half an hour. They had thirty minutes. For Kevin, it was a little more time to sleep; for John, time to lie here and enjoy the warmth of his body, the miracle of his breath, the beauty of his face. He had lived without all that for too long. He was going to appreciate every second he was given and pray that their time together would be measured in years rather than days.

TUESDAY NIGHT'S squall had blown itself out by Thursday morning, though the fair weather came with a drop in temperature. John could see his breath as they left the house through the back entrance. Kevin locked the french doors and fiddled with the remote that would disarm the garage alarms.

There were two separate garage alarms, one on the pedestrian door and the other on the lift-up hatch. Jones's crew had gone so far as to install a motion sensor on the car itself; even James Bond would've been satisfied with the precautions. But John still held his breath until Kevin backed the little blue coupe out into the alley.

"Keep an eye out for the delivery van," Kevin said as John climbed in. "That's our drag car. We'll be moving out behind a red Mini with a white top."

"A Mini?"

"You'd prefer an Aston Martin with an ejector seat?" Kevin chuckled. "Johnny, the whole point of camouflage is presenting a face that nobody really sees."

"You're going to be insufferable," John sighed. "I just knew it." His grousing was only a joke, and they both knew it. He was relieved and happy to be out in the open once more, even with lowering clouds threatening rain and a chance of snow, even with the potential danger.

"There's our nanny," Kevin said, as the little red car scooted down the street just before they turned out into traffic. "Don't forget, if another car gets close, check the driver's face."

"I know, I know." He was already doing exactly that—looking at every pedestrian, every parked car. This simple trip was planned with military precision; the local police had been warned of an antiterrorist action being conducted in Portsmouth, and if there was trouble, they could count on as much assistance as they could hope for.

"Here's our van," he told Kevin. He couldn't make out the driver, but as he squinted at the figure in the passenger seat, Sgt. Jones gave him a thumbs-up. "Papa Bear hard astern."

"I've read that male bears kill their offspring," Kevin said in a conversational tone.

"Well, you've said he's a rough customer."

Kevin chuckled. "I don't really care if you want to paint the kitchen white," he said unexpectedly.

John laughed. "I don't really care if you want yellow—if you really do. My gran always said yellow walls hide kitchen grease."

"My mother says yellow is good for the digestion."

"What?"

"She had acupuncture for something or other and read that in a book on Chinese medicine. Apparently yellow is good for the stomach. Don't ask me why."

John assimilated this bit of information. He thought Kevin's mother was a pretty sensible woman, but he didn't know what to make of that. "How can she tell?"

"Haven't a clue, Johnny. I can call her later if you're really curious, but it doesn't matter. We may as well just get the sample strips this time out. I was only thinking white does make sense since we don't know what sort of table we'll get, and white's neutral." He laughed. "When did I get so damned domestic?"

"I know what you mean. My old place was very beige, wasn't it? And I didn't give a damn. Until you turned up, home was just a place to eat, sleep, and study. Now it's everything." He put a hand on Kevin's leg, not wanting to distract him but needing the touch. "I'm glad you came back."

"So am I. It was funny, though, now I think about it. Even before the mission went to hell, I was getting restless. Maybe it's turning thirty—time to settle down, make a home for ourselves. Didn't seem much point to it just for myself, but with you it really matters."

The traffic picked up for a bit, so John turned his attention back to the other cars that passed them in the next lane. Three of them were driven by women, one by an older couple—midday in the middle of the week, that made sense and made his job as spotter a little easier.

They reached the DIY store without incident, and, after collecting enough paint samples to match anything in the Sistine

Chapel, took a quick run through the rest of the store. In the lighting department they found a floor lamp that was both inoffensive and had a nice fat clearance markdown. There was a bit of kitchen furniture on offer, but John didn't like the prices, and Kevin was certain his mother could direct them to a secondhand furniture shop that would have something better made and less expensive.

They could have lingered a lot longer—John spotted a computer station that had design software for remodeling work and thought they might make a model of Kevin's proposed attic renovation—but they decided to take pity on the two commandos stuck lurking amongst the plumbing supplies one aisle over. Still trailing their escort, they went through the checkout and got the bulky package safely back to Kevin's car. There was no fear that the vehicle had been tampered with, not with Jones and company in the van parked only a few spaces away.

A few minutes after they'd turned back onto the road, this time following the van and trailed by the Mini, Kevin's mobile beeped. "You boys need groceries?" the Sergeant inquired.

"I don't know. Kev, do we need groceries?"

"Doesn't matter," Jones said. "Turn in at Sainsbury's. There was a Mercedes pulled out a little too prompt behind you. I just want to make sure he keeps on going."

Another quick stop, this time for groceries, restored the Sergeant's peace of mind.

"Do you really think anyone would make a move this soon?" John asked after the second errand was accomplished.

"Not really." Kevin paused to let a courier van pass before pulling out of the car park. "But I'm damned sure Blackwell isn't going to send us an announcement. We can't let our guard down for a minute."

"I hope the bastard tries driving like an American and the police get him."

"It doesn't take that long to switch over," Kevin said. "I've done some right-hand driving. It's the left turns you have to watch."

"When was that?"

"A couple of years ago. I was part of a team sent to do cross-training in Canada."

"We could get married in Canada," John said thoughtfully. "Might be fun to see Niagara Falls."

"My mother would kill us. I know domestic partnership isn't quite the same, but that's how England would register a Canadian marriage, and Mum's already been hinting that she wants to throw a party."

John grinned. "I will *not* wear a long white dress."

"Damn right you won't," Kevin agreed. "I'd say plain dark suits, but I'd love to see you in proper dress clothes, for once."

"Let's let your mother decide." John was watching for traffic, trying to do his job, but the road was clear and quiet for the moment. "I don't know how your father's going to take all this, Kevin, but I love your mother."

"It's mutual," Kevin said. "When I told her about the new place, I found out that she'd never quite forgiven me for letting you get away the first time. If we couldn't get legal partnership, I think she'd just go ahead and adopt you. My sister's all for it, too. You've got a family now, like it or not."

"I like it a lot. I hope your brother can deal with it, when we break the news."

"I don't think he'll care one way or another. When I came out, he said he would take my share of the women. And if he can't handle it—well, I almost never see him except at Christmas. We'll need to make plans for that, too. Presents for the kids—chocolates or wine will do for the adults."

"I hope we're through this mess by then," John said. As they approached the deserted stretch of road where they'd rescued the kittens, he added, "You know, I miss the cats. I'm grateful your mum's keeping them safe, but I really miss them."

"So do I," Kevin said.

"You're joking."

"No. It's funny, I got used to them waking me up every morning. The house is too quiet without them. I didn't think I'd miss the crazy little buggers, but I—oh, *shit!*" He started to brake. "Johnny, check in, see if Jones can tell what's up."

Two cars had apparently disputed the right-of-way and collided in the middle of the crossroad less than a mile ahead. The road was blocked both ahead and to the left. John snatched the mobile phone from the seat between them just as it beeped.

"Looks routine, boys," the Sergeant said, "but I don't see either driver, and one of 'em looks like the car that followed you. No, wait—there's someone sitting beside the first car, left side of the road. I'm going around on the shoulder to the right. You follow me. There should be room if you go slow. Car two, if we get clear without interference, stop and offer assistance."

John relayed the instructions and rolled his window down, wondering if they ought to call an ambulance. No, Jones had probably taken care of that, or the men in car two would. There was no need for him to complicate anything; this team knew what it was doing.

"*Goddammit!*" Jones roared in his ear.

John jumped, jerked around, and saw that the delivery van had attempted to pass around the wrecked cars and somehow got stuck. It was tilted at an angle that suggested one wheel had dropped into an unseen ditch. Accidental, or a deliberately concealed deadfall? "What's going on?" John shouted, hearing a gunshot but unable to see where it was coming from.

"Trap! Turn right and drive on!"

His warning was unnecessary. As they got closer, the figure huddled beside the wrecked cars stood up with a gun in his hands and opened fire on the delivery van, joined by another gunman who'd apparently been hiding behind the second vehicle. The immobilized van was disgorging passengers, who took cover behind it and returned fire.

Kevin didn't need to be told anything. He made the obvious decision and swerved down the open, right-hand turn of the road, drove on for about a quarter-mile, then pulled over, dragged two combat helmets out of the backseat, and thrust one at John. They both rolled down their windows and leaned out, trying to see what was going on.

"He said to keep going," John shouted over the gunfire, though he would have done exactly what Kevin did.

Kevin shook his head. "No point. Six men in the van, two in the Mini. Unless there's a concealed ambush, they're outnumbered and outgunned." As he took the mobile from John, the little red car made the same turn and pulled off about twenty yards behind them. Two men got out, armed with automatic rifles. One ran off toward the firefight, the other jogged over to John's window.

"Yes," Kevin was saying to Jones. "Right. I'll call him now." He punched another button, paused. "Colonel? Yes, at the intersection. I see two shooters, there may be a third. No, I can't tell, no ID at this distance. Silver Mercedes, the other vehicle's tan or gold. Can't see enough to tell, it could be a Honda. Police and ambulance both, I think. And a wrecker to clear the cars from the right-of-way."

John was listening to the odd, one-sided conversation beside him with one ear while being instructed by the soldier from the Mini that they should stay where they were until the situation was under control. He obeyed, mainly because he couldn't very well open his door without knocking the man down.

"Yes," Kevin said on his right. "Yes, sir." He passed the phone to John, but leaned over to say, "Colonel for you, Washburn," to the soldier outside.

"Thank you, sir." Washburn took the instrument and moved a few feet back toward the battle, apparently relaying more specific information to his commanding officer.

"So it's over, then?" John asked, as the gunfire behind them died back to a couple of sporadic bursts, then stopped altogether.

"So it seems." Kevin was twisted in his seat, looking back toward the scene. He took John's hand and gave it a quick squeeze. "I hope so. But we won't know for certain unless Blackwell's in with that lot."

"I'd wondered if he might be working with anyone else." John felt very strange, almost dissociated. The neat manner in which they had been removed from the actual violence—in a way he was grateful for it, but in another way, it made the thing feel oddly unfinished.

"I don't know how he'd recruit anyone for such a brainless stunt," Kevin wondered. "Unless it was a total hoax—presenting himself as the government antiterrorist agent and making us out to be the villains."

"Better that than a whole gang out to get us," John said. The gunfire had ended; the acrid scent of cordite blew toward them on the chilly wind. But the same breeze was blowing the clouds apart, and the sudden winter sunshine was welcome.

Washburn came back and passed the phone to Kevin. "It's Sgt. Jones, sir."

"Thanks." Kevin listened for a moment. "What do you mean, you can't—yes, I can. I'll be right there."

"Now what?" John asked.

"I have to go check the casualties. Three shooters, all dead. Two of ours wounded."

"Blackwell?"

"Jones isn't sure. One of the casualties has a beard. It could be Blackwell—he fits the general description—but the Sergeant isn't buying it. He wants me to take a look." Kevin took the key out of the ignition and opened his door.

"Why not drive back?"

"Can't get through until they get a wrecker in. I'd like to know for certain that we've got him."

John nodded, smiling as his lover trotted off. As the emergency vehicle sirens began Dopplering closer, he considered how easily Kevin had slipped back into his command identity. John hoped he wouldn't miss this life too much. For himself, he wanted this to be the end of the adventure. The pistol on his belt, hidden under his long jacket, could go back to the Army without so much as a twinge of regret.

He climbed out of the car and followed at a distance. He didn't need to inspect the bodies. He had never met Blackwell in life, and he'd seen enough corpses to last a dozen lifetimes.

He could hear a siren coming up on him from behind and moved aside when he saw it was an ambulance. Odd, that. He'd have expected it to come from the Queen Alexandria hospital, off to the north. Perhaps they'd just been waiting along the road somewhere? Admirable response time, at any rate, but you couldn't say much for the driver's sense of caution. The driver was scowling. The driver—*what?*

John's body reacted before his mind could make sense of what he saw through the ambulance windscreen, and his sense of time went into crisis slow motion. As the screaming vehicle swept alongside and past him, Carl Blackwell at the wheel, John was already fumbling his pistol out of its holster, clicking the safety off, aiming for the tires of the vehicle that was swiftly closing in on his lover's unprotected back.

He squeezed off a shot, then another, then emptied the clip, screaming *"Kevin!"* as he fired. He knew at least one shot went home. He knew. He hoped.

For a long, terrible moment, nothing changed; the ambulance hurtled on. Kevin stopped and began to turn, moving too slowly to save himself even if he'd realized what was happening.

Then one of the tires blew out with a pop and another tire shredded, the steel-reinforced rubber peeling off in strips as the vehicle lurched, scraped along the roadway with a painful screech of wheel rim on pavement, and finally flipped over onto the driver's side, skidding off the road and into a ditch.

"It's Blackwell!" John shouted to Washburn, who was running toward the wreck. "Stay back!"

His hands shaking with adrenaline reaction, John found a second clip for the pistol and slapped it in to replace the empty one. He didn't think Blackwell would be conscious, but the rest of the team was too far away to help if he came out shooting.

"Johnny!" Kevin was suddenly beside him, mobile phone at his ear while he pulled John into a fierce hug with his free hand. "My God, I thought you'd run amok! Yes!" he said into the phone. "I don't know who you've got there, Sergeant, but send a few men over here if you can spare 'em. Blackwell was in the ambulance. I don't know what shape he's in, but if he's breathing, he's dangerous." He dropped the phone into his pocket and gave John a crooked, sidelong grin. "I don't ever want to hear you say you aren't the man I want watching my back."

If this had been a film, they'd have gone into a clinch, and the end credits would have rolled—but the job wasn't over yet. There was no sound or movement coming from the vehicle. That meant nothing; all three of them approached it with extreme caution, taking advantage of the blind-spot cover provided by the enclosed van's hull.

"There might be others in back," John said. "No one in the front passenger seat, though." And in hindsight, he realized that had been part of what had caught his attention—what was wrong with the picture. You never saw just one person in an empty ambulance. There were always two—the driver and an EMT. The mental snapshot was still sharp as a knife, that soulless killer's stare behind the wheel, focused on Kevin. Blackwell must have been so furious over his dismissal that he didn't care if he survived this attack. It was axiomatic—the hardest assassin to stop is one who is willing to die.

But maybe he hadn't intended suicide. Maybe he'd just meant to kill Kevin, drive off in the confusion, and abandon the vehicle, trusting to his luck to escape once again.

But his luck had run out. It was over.

"I can't believe I could've been that stupid," Kevin said as they closed on the van's back door. "He did what I knew he'd do—waited till I dropped my guard. I knew it. And I did it anyway."

"We knew he'd used a stolen car, love," John said. "Who in their right mind would expect a stolen ambulance?"

"And who was it telling you to watch for the vehicles nobody ever sees? You should kick my arse. Emergency services—the last thing anyone would think of." He dropped to his knees at the outside edge of the van and picked up a shard of the broken rearview mirror, angling it to check the cargo compartment. "Empty," he said, and risked a look through the window that had broken out. "No one back here."

"I don't want to *kick* your arse," John said under his breath, as he leaned down to confirm Kevin's observation.

Kevin looked up, blue eyes like a lighthouse beacon. "I wish I could kiss you," he answered, too low for Washburn to hear. His voice tingled all the way down to John's toes.

"Not in front of the children," John chided. "We don't want to alarm them—they're heavily armed."

He gave Kevin a hand up as they both edged around to the passenger door at the front of the van. Kevin tossed the bit of mirror to Washburn, on the van's other side, and he used it to check the front compartment through the windscreen.

"I think he's unconscious, sir," he reported. "Possibly dead."

"Keep him covered," Kevin said. "Door locked?"

It was, and before they could do anything by way of breaking through the windscreen or shooting open the lock, Jones and two of his men had arrived. The road-blocking accident had been a sham; both cars were drivable, and Jones's men had cleared them out of the road. The civilians, specifically Mr. Kendrick and Mr. Hanson, were politely but firmly encouraged to return to their vehicle and go home.

John was happy to comply and was perfectly willing to remind Kevin that the only place he was seriously needed was at his partner's side. There was no way he was going to kiss Kev in front of all those commandos, but no way he was going to make it back home without a minute or two of privacy.

He tossed his helmet into the backseat. "Wait," he said, as Kevin put the key in the ignition. "And take that stupid thing off your head."

The first touch of Kevin's lips hit him like an electric shock. John forgot about breathing, didn't care. They couldn't get close enough with all the clothing and the damned vests, and it was a little car and the bloody gearshift console stuck up between them. It was the gearshift giving him a nasty jab in the balls that convinced John they just couldn't shag in the front seat of a compact car.

"Home," Kevin gasped. "Let's go home."

"Good."

"And don't touch me, or we'll wind up in a ditch."

"Then get us home fast."

Chapter Seventeen

THEY'D GOT themselves under tenuous control by the time they reached home and put the car away. By way of distraction, Kevin explained that he'd recognized the casualties from the ambush—they were the three other members of Blackwell's original squad who had also dropped out of sight. How they'd managed to get into the country was anyone's guess, but figuring that out was Immigration's headache.

John blinked when Kevin rang the doorbell instead of simply using his key, but understood when the door was opened by a soldier wearing the coveralls of a carpet-installation firm. Kevin introduced them both, asked whether the team had been informed of developments—they had—then thanked them and shut the door behind them with a look of unbelievable relief.

John wrapped his lover in the kind of whole-body embrace he hadn't dared attempt in public, and Kevin relaxed against him. The feeling was almost beyond words. Safe, whole, free of the sense of impending disaster. "It's over," he said.

Kevin nodded, turning his face to kiss the side of John's neck. "Yes." His hands slipped under John's sweater and began undoing the straps of the bulky body armor. "Now, what was it you wanted to do to my arse? 'Not kicking' is a little vague. Can you be more specific?"

"Come upstairs and I'll show you." John's legs were a little longer, and that gave him the advantage in getting upstairs in a hurry. But Kevin was right behind him, and in thirty seconds, they were on the bed, a trail of shed clothing marking their progress down the hall.

John rolled onto his back, pulling Kevin over on top of him, delighting in the solid heat of skin against naked skin. He held Kev close as they kissed, Kevin's arm supporting his head as he let his hands down over his lover's back and lower, to that beautiful, tight little rear. He didn't have room in his head for a thought of what he was going to do about that, though, because their bodies pressed so tightly together that his overheated cock was trapped against Kevin's. It was like that first night, only better; he couldn't ask for more. And from the way Kevin was beginning to thrust against him, they were on the same wavelength.

What did he want to do? Silly question. Squeeze, and thrust, and savor the sweet mouth joined so deeply to his own, the intensity of pleasure running through his body like a spring tide. So good, so wonderful, and he'd come so close to losing it all—

He squeezed hard, maybe too hard, but Kevin only gasped and writhed against him, breaking the kiss to pull in a huge shuddering breath. John slid a finger between his cheeks, sliding inside, and Kev arched wildly, crying out. That sound, as always, pushed John over the top as well.

Kevin rolled off to one side, his blue eyes slightly unfocused, and John pulled him close as they both relaxed into the afterglow.

"Excellent answer," Kevin said when he got his breath back.

"That—actually, that wasn't what I'd had in mind," John admitted.

Kevin started to laugh.

"No, really—" Apparently that was just as funny and set off another round of chuckles. "Well, all right, then." He reached out a foot, hooked his T-shirt off the corner of the bed, and used it to wipe them off. By that time Kevin's mirth had subsided. "I'm glad to make you so happy," John said finally. "Would you like a shower, or shall we just stay here for a bit?"

Kevin pulled him back down. "This for now," he said. "Though I think we should think about something to eat before too long."

"Mmm. You mean actual food, or going for seconds?"

"You randy devil," Kevin said affectionately. "I meant actual food, but not just yet." He pulled the duvet back up onto the bed—somehow it had been kicked aside—and over them both. But he didn't seem able to rest contentedly. After shifting position three times, he finally raised up on one elbow. "Johnny."

"What?"

"It's too quiet. We need to go get the cats."

"Now? Today?"

"Why not?"

John let his head drop back on the pillow for what he suspected was the last bit of downtime he'd have for the rest of the day. "Well, it's nearly four in the afternoon, we'll hit the worst of the evening traffic, and it'll take hours to reach your parents' house. And once we're there, your mother isn't going to let us leave until she's tried some new recipe—" He stopped and reconsidered what he'd just said.

"You see my point?" Kevin asked. "It would be different if Mum were one of those horror cooks who never gets anything right, but she almost never gets anything wrong. And if we go tonight, we won't have to deal with my father—he's off to Scotland about some golf resort and won't be home until Saturday. But he's bound to be pleased to come home and find our cats out of his hair." He settled against John's shoulder and made himself comfortable. "Still, it's up to you. I just thought you'd like to have everything sorted."

John rested his chin against Kevin's hair and sighed. This was so good. Nearly perfect.

But Kevin was right. It was too damned quiet.

IT WAS two in the morning by the time they made it back home. Kevin had endured several hours of cat opera, which had gone a long way toward making him reconsider the wisdom of his idea. He had forgotten how much the kittens hated to travel—and how loudly they voiced their objections.

He had received a follow-up call from the Colonel on their way back that answered their few remaining questions, and he took a perverse delight in his former superior's complaints about the audio interference. Though with the cat-racket going on, he hadn't tried to relay the information to John until they were home and soaking in a scented, bubbling tub.

Blackwell had survived the crash with only minor injuries. Believing himself to be above legal prosecution, the mercenary had been willing to explain to the Colonel how he had managed to find the house in Portsmouth so quickly.

He had followed the men of Kevin's former troop.

"I don't think the old man has ever been so embarrassed," Kevin said, scooping Emma off the edge of the tub and handing Johnny a towel. "All that cloak-and-dagger bullshit about our security, and the bastard followed Jones here when he delivered all those toys to keep us safe."

"Well, it was a time-saver, wasn't it?" John toweled himself dry. "God knows how long we'd have been stuck here otherwise."

"I know, Johnny, but… wouldn't you expect people who deal with military intelligence to have just a little common sense?"

"No. They get distracted by their own drama. Turn around. I'll dry your back."

Kevin leaned against the shower wall and enjoyed the pampering. "Now, a question for you," John said. "What do you want rubbed first? Feet? Back? Other parts?"

"Everything?" Kevin said hopefully as the cats followed them back to the bedroom.

"Greedy bugger. But all right—if you tell me what they've done with this Blackwell bastard. Does he really know where so many bodies are buried that the law can't touch him?"

"That depends on what you mean by 'the law.'" Kevin stretched out and propped his feet up on John's lap. "The US doesn't want him back—too embarrassing, particularly since he'd have to be tried for murdering a British Army officer, and serve whatever sentence he'd get, before we would extradite him. They know he's probably responsible for the murder over there, but they don't have any evidence. And the British Army doesn't want to drag him out and uncork the cesspool all over again. Fine with me—I would have to testify against him, and I've had my fill of the spotlight."

"So…?" John prompted.

"So, there is another jurisdiction that has a previous claim on extradition. That claim is going to be honored, very discreetly, so instead of the deportation Blackwell expects, he's going to be sent back to a little town in the Middle East where he's wanted for murder."

John whistled. "That's going to be a short trial."

"And no need to consider extradition afterwards. The Colonel asked me for a deposition when I declined to go back and testify. I don't know if the other men will go—probably not. I expect the government wants to keep a very low profile on the whole affair. But he'll get a trial, and the family will get justice. I saw Blackwell commit that murder—there's no doubt of his guilt."

John hesitated, and Kevin knew what he was going to say. "Do you want to go testify in person?"

"Christ, no, Johnny. I never want to go back there again. And before you start worrying, it's not because you don't want me to. I'm sick of the whole damned thing. I'm just glad it's over."

John poured sandalwood oil into his palm and began working it into one of Kevin's very clean feet. "Thanks, love. And what about this consulting contract? Any further obligations?"

It was very difficult to think with Johnny making him feel so good. "None. In lieu of a fee, they're letting us keep the alarms they installed. I may do clearance-level translating as an independent contractor—there's always a shortage of reliable translators—but no more field work."

"Even better. I think you know how much I appreciate that."

John switched to the other foot, and Kevin felt himself melting into a puddle. "It can't be as much as I appreciate this. You have golden hands."

"And they go so well with your silver tongue."

"Johnny, put the cap on the bottle and lie down, would you?"

"What about the rest of your massage?"

"I want to massage your parts with my parts. And if I don't do it soon, I'm going to fall asleep."

"Love, you're already falling asleep. And so am I."

"Mm. I think you're right." He wanted to look at the clock, but his eyelids were incredibly heavy. "What time is it, anyway?"

"Three a.m."

"First thing in the morning, then."

"Fair enough." He felt Johnny reach across him to switch off the light, pull the covers over them both, and snuggle down beside him. A small furry body parked itself just under his chin and started to buzz. The other kitten marched up his leg, purred in his ear for a few seconds, then wandered off to nest somewhere on John's side of the blanket.

He felt one more thing—a kiss on the back of his neck—and then fell into a deep and dreamless sleep.

The years go by. The world moves forward.

2014

"CALLING THE old man?"

Caught in the act with his hand on the phone, there was nothing Kevin could do but nod and say, "Yes. That is, if I can get up the nerve to actually do it." Did he need to tell John that he had been at this point at least a dozen times already, only to have his nerve fail? No, he did not.

He was enveloped in warmth as Johnny wrapped both arms around him from behind. "I'm glad," he said. "I understand why you left it this long, but—"

"Can't put it off any longer, or I'll be reporting after the fact." He left the phone in the cradle and turned, catching his breath at the sight. Fully dressed, John Hanson's curly mop of dark hair, deep brown eyes, and sensuous mouth were distracting enough. In nothing but snug, rainbow-striped briefs, his slim, leggy body was trouble on two bare feet.

Kevin pushed him away, holding him at arms' length. Any other time, he'd have pulled John over to the sofa and to hell with their schedule, but not today. They hadn't a moment to spare. "I can do it myself, Johnny. For God's sake, go put your clothes on. The worst the Brig can do is disown me, but if we're late for this, you'll never get another meal from my mother."

"You know me too well." John swooped in for a quick kiss, then loped off upstairs.

"And for God's sake, change those pants!" Kevin called after him, knowing that even if John heard that order, he'd ignore it. No harm in that, really. John spent much of his time doing crisis counseling; if his silly underwear gave him something to smile about, more power to it. It wouldn't show under the formal attire anyway, and it would be fun to help him take it off, later....

Kevin shook his head. He was stalling and he knew it. He'd faced gunfire, terrorists, disgrace, and a very determined murderer, but he would sooner tackle any or all of them at once than make this call. He must do it now, right this minute; he didn't have time for cold feet. They had to finish dressing, pick up the elderly lady who'd been John's surrogate grandmother since he'd moved to Portsmouth, and present themselves at the registry office with a little time to spare in case of last-minute complications.

He picked up the phone again and punched the number one deliberate digit at a time, even though it was loaded into speed dial. *What can he do, after all—jump through the receiver and throttle me?*

He might want to.

The call was answered after two and a half rings. A strong voice, brusque, accustomed to command. "Kendrick."

"Hi, Dad."

"Kevin." A pause, as though the Brigadier was trying to guess why his younger son had called. "Your mother's not here. She's off at the hall, supervising the caterer for your friend's reception. I'm to meet her there in ninety minutes."

Mrs. Kendrick had suggested this explanation, and it was not entirely false; Pat and Tess were tying the knot this morning too. Tess's mother had never been able to accept that her daughter's partner was a woman, and she had flatly refused to have anything to do with their ceremony. Kevin's mother, who liked nothing better than a family wedding, had flung herself into the breach. Since Kevin was the biological father of the very pregnant bride's unborn baby—their second—the two couples had decided to combine festivities.

But no one had told Brigadier General Marcus D. Kendrick (Retired) the whole story. He had always been inclined to the Yank policy of "don't ask, don't tell" with regard to his younger son's love life, and did not even—officially—know Kevin was gay.

"Yes," Kevin said. "I know. I meant to call you." Damn it, he had no reason to be nervous. His father was a forceful man, not an ogre, and he was, after all, many miles away. "Dad, I just wanted you to know that John and I are having our own wedding ceremony today, and—" He held the phone away from his ear. He'd never heard anyone make that sound before. "Dad?"

"You. Are. *What*?"

"Getting married, Dad. The law changed a while back. We're in the twenty-first century. Rainbow over Parliament, remember?"

Silence. But he could hear breathing. A good sign, very good—the old man hadn't keeled over.

Kevin plowed ahead. "I didn't tell you earlier because it's not open for discussion, but I'm not going to sneak around behind your back."

"But—" Another long silence, then, "*Why*, Kevin? Damn it, I guessed as much, but why bother? Can't you just—do whatever it is you do—without—"

"Of course we could." Kevin felt a twinge of pain in his hand and realized how hard he was clutching the receiver. "Of course we could, Dad. But do you remember what you told me about this? I couldn't have been more than twelve or thirteen. I forgot all about it until just now. Guess it made an impression."

"Told you what?"

"That when I found the right one, I should grab hold with both hands and make it permanent. Make it real, you said. Be a man. Give your word and honor it."

"I was talking about a real marriage, boy. A home, children. Not some—"

"Yes. Exactly. So am I." God, interrupting his father twice. He didn't know if he'd ever done that before. "The real thing. I know it's not what you wanted or expected, and I'll understand if I don't see you there. But this is who I am—who I love—and I'm not going to hide it." He sensed John's warmth behind him once more, felt stronger for his presence. "That's all, Dad. Sorry I didn't tell you sooner, but I didn't think you really wanted to know. Take care."

He fumbled as he put the receiver down with an unsteady hand. Adrenaline hangover; he turned blindly into John's embrace and just held on. Eventually he was breathing normally again.

"Think he'll be there?" John asked.

"I don't know, Johnny." Kevin took a deep breath and raised his head, meeting the eyes of the man he loved. Lover. Partner. Husband. He felt lighter somehow, almost giddy. "That's up to him. If he doesn't accept you as a son-in-law, it's his loss. Have you got the rings?"

"I do." John grinned in delight. "Just rehearsing my line. Come on, love—get us to the registry office on time."

Epilogue

"SEE MUMMY!" Patricia Kevyn Sullivan-Chalton—named for her biological mother's wife and her biological father's husband—was an enchantingly lovely child, with her mother's red-gold hair and her father's dark eyes. But it was anyone's guess where she got her obstinate disposition or her piercing voice, which echoed tremendously in the lift. None of her parents were especially loud, and there was no genetic reason for the stubbornness.

"Yes, love," Kevin agreed. "We're going to see your mummy and your mum, and if you're very good and quiet, we'll take you out for lunch afterward and buy you a nice dosa." The promise of a thin, rolled pancake from their favorite Indian place usually did the trick.

Not today. "No!"

"Pattycake, your mummy worked very hard making you a baby brother, and she needs for you to be a good girl and not shout."

"Don't want brother, want Mummy!"

John had been honored that Pat and Tess had asked him to be the biological father of their child, and thrilled that they'd asked Kevin to pitch in for the second baby. And he was also profoundly grateful that the ladies were doing all the child-rearing. He loved his daughter, even though he was more than a bit uneasy when she was in his and Kevin's care.

She was sweet—when she wasn't trying to rule the world—and it had been amazing to watch her develop from a helpless pink infant to a very small person with a very large force of character. He suspected that when she grew old enough to speak in sentences that did not feature "no!" as a constant refrain, he would feel less stressed by prolonged exposure and the 24/7 responsibility. They had never been able to put P. K. down for the night with any hope that she would sleep more than a couple of hours. He had no idea how Pat and Tess managed day to day, or what unfathomable optimism had prompted them to want a second baby.

It might simply be that his own disposition was not rugged enough to endure prolonged exposure to very small children—at least not this small child. Maybe it was that he'd had no siblings himself—the upheaval didn't seem to bother Kevin nearly as much. The past two days that she'd been staying with them, while her mothers were occupied with the birth of their second child, had been two of the most nerve-wracking days of his life since—well, since that ex-mercenary maniac had come after Kevin.

"Sweetheart—" John was trying to be the adult in the situation, but his daughter had an uncanny ability to neutralize all his professional training. Somehow or other, she knew he wanted her to settle down before the lift opened on the maternity ward, and she wasn't having any.

"Johnny, there's a reason they call 'em the 'terrible twos.'" Kevin scooped up the toddler and looked her in the eye. "P. K., you are a very smart little girl."

"Yes!"

"And you know how to behave, don't you?"

She narrowed her eyes suspiciously, but Kevin gave her a wink and a big grin, which set her laughing, and when the lift opened it showed only a cheery family group.

John breathed a sigh of relief.

"And since you're such a good girl, you can be a *good* big sister, like your aunt Marian," Kevin continued, holding the child's attention. "Can you do that, honey?"

P. K. nodded. "I'm good. I want Mummy. Want Mum."

"Which way, Johnny?"

John tucked the bouquet of roses under his arm, checked the slip of paper, looked at the plaque on the wall, and pointed to the left. They headed down the hospital corridor, with P. K. softly chanting "Mummy, Mummy, Mummy...."

"How can it still be terrible twos?" John asked under his breath. "She's nearly three!"

"She got a late start with the diva act. Making up for lost time."

They found the room, whisked her inside, and got the door shut before she shrieked again, as they knew she would. But she listened to her mum, Pat, and settled down enough to be lifted up to get a hug from her mummy, Tess, while the adults exchanged their own greetings and John handed over the flowers. It had been well worth the extra expense, which he and Kevin had insisted on paying, to have this private room for the day or two Tess would need it.

"Has she been much trouble?" Pat asked, as Tess reassured the little girl that, yes, Mummy loved her and she was Mum's very favorite daughter.

"No more than usual," Kevin said. "I think the cats are a bit overwrought, but they'll recover."

"Where's the baby?" John asked. "In the nursery?"

"No, if the baby's healthy, they stay in the room now. Over here." She led them around to the crib behind the pull-away curtain. "We thought we'd give Peek a few minutes with Tess first. He's sleeping. Isn't he just the most beautiful little boy you ever saw?"

Douglas John Sullivan-Chalton was a tiny, red-faced creature who bore no particular resemblance to his handsome father. He looked as squished and homely as any normal newborn. But looking at the pride and happiness on Kevin's face, John saw beauty enough for a thousand babies. "He's gorgeous. Is Tess all right?"

"I told you on the phone, John. She's fine. A little tired, still— thanks for waiting till this afternoon to come by. It was easier than with P. K., actually. Just a couple of hours in labor. The midwife was thrilled."

"He's so tiny," Kevin said, running a finger along the back of the little pink fist that rested on the flannel blanket. "Are you sure he's all right?"

"Seven pounds, seven ounces. He's a fine, healthy boy." As if in confirmation, the baby's eyes opened, and he waved the little fist and kicked at his blanket. "Would you like to hold him?"

Kevin, with considerable experience as an uncle, had been perfectly at ease with P. K. when she was an infant. But this time he hesitated. "Are you sure?"

"Pick up your son, Kevin," Tess said from the other side of the curtain. "John, can you push this thing back? Pattycake, would you like to see your new baby brother?"

"Mine?"

"Yes." Pat scooped up the baby and transferred him carefully to Kevin's arms, then went over to hug her daughter and give her wife a kiss. "Yours, and mine, and Mummy's, and your daddies' too. He's all of ours. And we're his family."

"Can he play ball with me?" P. K. asked.

"He's got to grow bigger before he can play with you," John said. "Give him some time. But we'll take you out and play ball in a little while."

"He's awfully quiet," Kevin said, still staring at little Douglas as though he expected the baby to do something bizarre.

"A woman in our Lamaze class said the second baby is always the complete opposite of the first," Tess said with a huge yawn. "I hope she's right—a restful baby would be wonderful."

P. K. was watching the new baby, and her mother, and Kevin. She said tentatively, "I'm wonderful, too?"

"Sweetie, you were a wonderful, *exciting* baby," Pat said. "Full of surprises. We hope Dougie will be a wonderful, *calm* baby."

"Hear, hear," John agreed. "Ladies, he's beautiful. You do good work."

"Couldn't have done it without you," Tess said, smiling at Kevin.

"I'm—thank you for asking me," Kevin said. "Both of you." He had been so surprised when they'd asked him to be the father of Tess's second baby and completely devastated when the pregnancy failed. He hadn't expected them to ask him when they were ready to try again. But the same thing had happened with their first attempt, so the ladies simply persisted. John didn't understand the drive for parenthood, but seeing Kevin this way, he was glad they had carried on.

"It was too perfect," Pat said. "Since my dad's name is John, too, we could get both your names and Tess's dad."

"I didn't care about the name," John said. And he meant it, even though he was absurdly pleased at P. K.'s middle name, despite the silly spelling. "This being Kevin's baby—I couldn't ask for more."

"I'm afraid I can, though," Tess said. "I'm just about ready to have a kip, but I have to feed the baby first...."

"And we need to feed his big sister." John held out his arms for P. K. "Come on, young lady."

She launched herself into his embrace and leaned over toward Kevin. "That's my baby!"

"Your baby brother. Yes." He took a couple of steps closer so P. K. could get a good look at the new arrival, hoping sibling rivalry wasn't going to rear its ugly head.

But she behaved as well as anyone could expect of a toddler a month shy of her third birthday. She patted the little hand, much as Kevin had done. "My baby brother." Then she patted Kevin's face. "My daddy."

"Hey," John said. "What about me?"

More pats. "Daddy too!"

"That works." Kevin leaned over and gave John a kiss, light and sweet. P. K. laughed and patted them both. Then she had to give Kevin a kiss, and John as well—she had learned that adults really didn't like a big sloppy smack on the nose, so she delighted in giving them—and then both her mothers, and then the baby. And then Kevin handed the baby over to Tess for his midafternoon snack, and they left young Dougie to lunch with the ladies.

"I was good!" P. K. announced. And she had been, for such a little girl, so they played the game she took such delight in—holding on to either hand and assisting her in taking long, leaping steps along the pavement as they strolled off to find some lunch on a bright April afternoon.

"This is how you'd step if you were walking on the moon," Kevin told her. "If you were an astronaut."

"Careful what you ask for," John cautioned.

"Well, she could be an astronaut. Why not? She's strong and smart—aren't you, Miss Peek?"

"Yes! I can count to a hundred!" And she began to demonstrate. "One. Two. Three. Four...." She couldn't really reach one hundred—she just knew it was an important number. She was pretty accurate up to twenty, though. "Nine. Ten. 'Leven. Twelve...."

"I'd be scared out of my mind, that's why not."

"Ah, Johnny...." Kevin looked as happy as John had ever seen him. "We could have grandkids living on the moon, did you ever think of that? Sometimes things work out. Look at us. You've got your practice, I've got the translating and the books—we've got our house and the kids.... Four years ago, did you ever imagine life could be this good?"

John looked over at his lover—his husband—above the bouncing head of their little girl, who had just transposed twenty-six and twenty-seven. His thoughts flew back to that cold, bleak day in November when he picked up the telephone and sunlight came back into his life.

Before he'd met Kevin, he had lived on autopilot, and his best friends were those he found on the library shelves. Now he had the love of his life, a reason for living, and a family he had never even thought to wish for. This wasn't anything like what he'd imagined. It was a hundred times better, maybe a thousand.

"No, love. No. I never did."

Kevin smiled back, and John could see the promise of their next night alone together in his eyes. "You know something, Johnny? Neither did I."

Afterword

IN EARLIER editions of *Walking Wounded*, I left hints about John and Kevin's previous incarnation together. Dreamspinner decided that they should come out of the closet, so… as those who've read the Royal Navy series may have guessed, these two souls were once known as David Archer and William Marshall, and they earned the right to a lifetime where they could be together openly, without fear.

Or—if reincarnation seems a bit too far-fetched for you—just think of it as a story about two young men in the early years of the twenty-first century who coincidentally happen to live in Portsmouth, England.

The references to past-life regression work are real—I'm a certified hypnotherapist myself and have taken training in the specialty. If you're interested, I'd be happy to share a list of the books I've read and learned from. Just write to lee.rowan@yahoo.com.

Keep reading for an excerpt from

Ransom

Royal Navy: Book One

By Lee Rowan

An officer, a gentleman... and a sodomite. The first two earn him honor and respect, the third may cost him his life. David Archer realizes how hopeless his attraction to his fellow midshipman is from the moment a newly-arrived William Marshall challenges a sexually abusive shipmate to a duel—and shoots him dead.

To Marshall, the Navy is his one chance to move beyond his humble beginnings. While others spend shore leave carousing, he curls up with a navigation text. When they and their captain are abducted, Archer and Marshall become pawns in a renegade's sadistic game. To protect the man he loves, David Archer chooses to face his own demons of past abuse returned in a different form. When Marshall learns of Archer's sacrifice, he discovers what he feels for Davy runs stronger and deeper than friendship. He's in love, for the first time in his life, and he wants to know all about this new emotion.

But first they must escape. Only then will they find out if they can preserve their love without losing their lives.

http://www.dreamspinnerpress.com

Prologue

Plymouth, England, June 1796

TWO MEN in midshipmen's uniform—the elder burly and red-faced, the younger slim and deathly pale—stood back-to-back in a sunny glade not far from Plymouth harbor. Each held a pistol in his right hand. The warm breeze and sylvan loveliness around them were lost on both the combatants and the three onlookers.

One of those three raised his voice. "Mr. Correy, Mr. Marshall.... Gentlemen, you are certain you cannot be reconciled?"

"Oh, I could be, easily," said the larger man. "Mr. Marshall knows well that I would be happy to make our acquaintance a closer one."

"No," said Marshall. He bit his lip and pushed a stray lock of black hair behind his ear. "Impossible."

"Very well," said the referee, who was also surgeon of the ship *Titan*, on which they all served. "Take ten paces."

They did.

"On the count of three, turn and fire. One. Two. Three."

Both turned quickly; the shots sounded as one. After a moment, the larger man toppled slowly to one side. By the time the surgeon reached him, he had breathed his last.

"Best clear out before someone comes," said Correy's second, who was purser of their ship. The others agreed, then carried the dead man to the carriage in which he had arrived. The surgeon and purser climbed aboard.

"What—what happens now?" Marshall asked. For all his earlier resolve, he was now clearly anxious about the possible consequences of his victory.

The surgeon shook his head. "Lad," he said, rather kindly, "you've not been aboard *Titan* long, have you?"

"Only since last week."

"Then my guess is Captain Cooper will be pleased to log that Mr. Correy died in a duel with an unknown landsman. And if Correy's family is wise, they'll let it go at that. Every man aboard knew his habits, but he was too clever to leave evidence."

"You've done the ship a service," the purser said. "Begone, now. And clean your pistol." He took up the reins and clucked to the horse. In a moment the carriage disappeared from view.

"Mr. Archer," Marshall said to the young man beside him. "Is he serious?"

"Yes, completely. Come, sir, he was right, we must be off." They climbed into the light trap they'd hired in town, and Archer skillfully guided the horse back onto the roadway.

Marshall was silent for a long time. "I… have never killed in cold blood before," he said at last. "Nor ever killed an Englishman." He turned and met Archer's eyes, looking for an instant like the eighteen-year-old boy he was rather than the correct officer and gentleman he had been while facing death. "Tell me, Mr. Archer— what else could I have done?"

"Nothing," Archer said. He had liked Marshall from the moment the new midshipman came aboard the *Titan,* even though Marshall's time in the service gave him seniority over Archer himself. That immediate affinity was part of the reason he had agreed to act as Marshall's second in this affair; his new shipmate was all alone, but that hadn't stopped him from standing up to a bully. "The man was a menace, Mr. Marshall. He made life hell for any boy above the age of consent. Younger than fourteen, a boy could charge rape, so he let the children alone. Older, the victim dared not speak—he could be hanged himself, for participating."

"In the first place…." Marshall still seemed to be trying to convince someone, most likely himself, that he'd been in the right. "In the first place, the Articles of War specifically forbid sodomy between men, on penalty of death."

"Indeed."

"I've never—I have served three years in His Majesty's Navy, Mr. Archer. On a sloop, to be sure, and under a strict Captain. I know all men have human weaknesses, but I have never seen such a blatant disregard for common decency!"

"I believe Captain Cooper has been in an awkward position," Archer said. "He knew Correy was untrustworthy, but the man was clever and deceitful. He bribed the men under his command to act as his spies and lookouts, and Correy's family has influence enough to lose Cooper his command if he had acted without ironclad evidence. The Captain did the best he could to keep Correy from power—he never made him Acting Lieutenant, nor recommended him for the Lieutenant's examination."

"His family must have been influential indeed, for him to flout the Articles," Marshall replied. "How could he make such a proposition, bald-faced, and even threaten me? To claim he'd had a boy flogged for refusing him—!"

"He did, more or less," Archer said. "Correy made his wishes known, the boy refused, so he brought the boy before the Captain and charged that the youngster had made the proposition. The boy was so flustered he must have appeared guilty of something. The Captain had him caned, not flogged, for 'unclean behavior.'"

"What!"

"He had to do something. Correy swore on the Bible, and all the boy could do was deny he'd done anything. At least there's no death penalty for it. And refusing didn't even help the lad. Correy had his way with him eventually, poor little bastard."

"My God." Marshall let out a long breath. "Thank you for telling me that, Mr. Archer. I will not speak of this to anyone, but you have eased my conscience."

Archer smiled. "You have made the *Titan* a safer place for our youngsters, sir. It is I who should thank you."

They drove on again in silence. Marshall seemed at ease, but Archer's spirit was now in turmoil. His gratitude was far deeper than that of a concerned officer. Marshall had freed him from a demon who had made his existence a living hell.

He had not told Marshall that the boy he spoke of had been himself.

And Archer had not, and never could, tell Marshall that he just had fallen in love with a brave and beautiful gentleman who would likely shoot him dead if he ever gave voice to his feelings.

Winds of Change & Eye of the Storm

Royal Navy: Book Two

By Lee Rowan

Winds of Change

Lieutenants William Marshall and David Archer, of His Majesty's frigate Calypso, have been lovers for more than a year. Because the penalty for discovery is the hangman's noose, they limit themselves to the occasional night of passion ashore.

But in the Navy, nothing lasts forever. A transfer to a new ship brings with it a bizarre turn of events: their captain orders them to behave as though they are involved in an illicit relationship in order to smoke out a suspected traitor. When their masquerade proves dangerously effective, it threatens to cost Davy his life.

Eye of the Storm

The long war between England and France enters a fragile and temporary truce in the winter of 1802, but the lives of Commander William Marshall and Lieutenant David Archer are more complicated than ever. After almost losing Davy in battle, Will faces the responsibility of command and questions whether he can give orders that will put his love in harm's way once more.

Doubts torment David Archer. Will walked away once, trying to end their relationship for Davy's own safety. His physical wounds have healed, but the loss of trust remains. Now, his biggest challenge is persuading Will their love is worth the risk of loss.

http://www.dreamspinnerpress.com

Home is the Sailor

Royal Navy: Book Three

By Lee Rowan

The Royal Navy meets the Stately English Manor Murder Mystery, and if it were only a matter of Colonel Mustard in the library, things would be so much easier.

After an ambush by the French while on a routine surveillance mission, Will Marshall and David Archer are advised to retreat to the English countryside to avoid Bonaparte's animosity for a time. Upon their arrival, they discover that David's eldest brother has died after a mysterious accident and this puts his other, very unsuitable brother in line for the title. David's suspicions—that the new heir had a hand in his brother's death—seem so unreasonable that even Will finds it difficult to believe his fears are valid. If Davy thought his lover was hard to convince, his autocratic father, who still sees him as the inept youngest son, won't even listen to him. Davy and Will are thrust into the role of sleuths, trying to determine the truth behind the mystery.

All the while Will has concerns of his own: his fear of losing Davy is still stronger than his desire to keep Davy beside him on the quarterdeck… but he knows no other life than the Navy.

http://www.dreamspinnerpress.com

Sail Away

Royal Navy: Book Four

By Lee Rowan

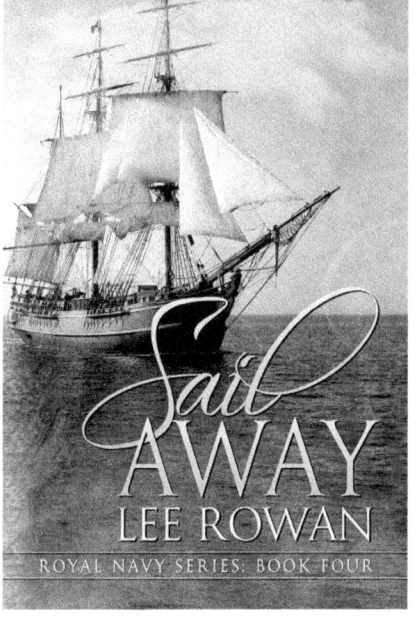

Sail away again with Will Marshall and Davy Archer in this collection of missing moments from their saga. Meet some of the background players as they take center stage in tales of their own. Enjoy a journey through the family album of the Royal Navy series in the following stories:

Captain's Courtship is the tale of Cynthia Lancaster and newly promoted Commander Paul Smith, who won't let revolution stand in the way of their love.

David Archer's cousin Christopher St. John and his fiancée wind up on the *HMS Calypso* in *See Paris and Live*.

When a storm leaves Will and David *Castaway* on a deserted island, their fantasy is within reach… if they dare to take the chance.

After the harrowing events in *Ransom*, Will Marshall realizes the vast difference between their social standing in their *Voyage to London*, and he wonders whether there will be room in Davy's life for him after all.

Finally, enjoy six short Royal Navy stories that show a glimpse of Will and Davy at the holidays—Halloween, Christmas, Valentine's day, shore leave… and a special nit-picking vignette from Charlie Cochrane.

http://www.dreamspinnerpress.com

LEE ROWAN has been writing since childhood, but professionally only since spring of 2006, with the publication of her Eppie-winning novel, *Ransom*. She is a lady of a certain age, old enough to know better but still young enough to do it anyway. A confirmed bookaholic with a wife of many years, she is kept in line by a cadre of cats and two dogs who get her away from the computer and out of the house at least once a day.

DANCE OFF

ARIEL TACHNA & NESSA L. WARIN

http://www.dreamspinnerpress.com

Chasing the
Swallows

JOHN INMAN

http://www.dreamspinnerpress.com

Dirk Hunter

AFTER SCHOOL ACTIVITIES

http://www.dreamspinnerpress.com

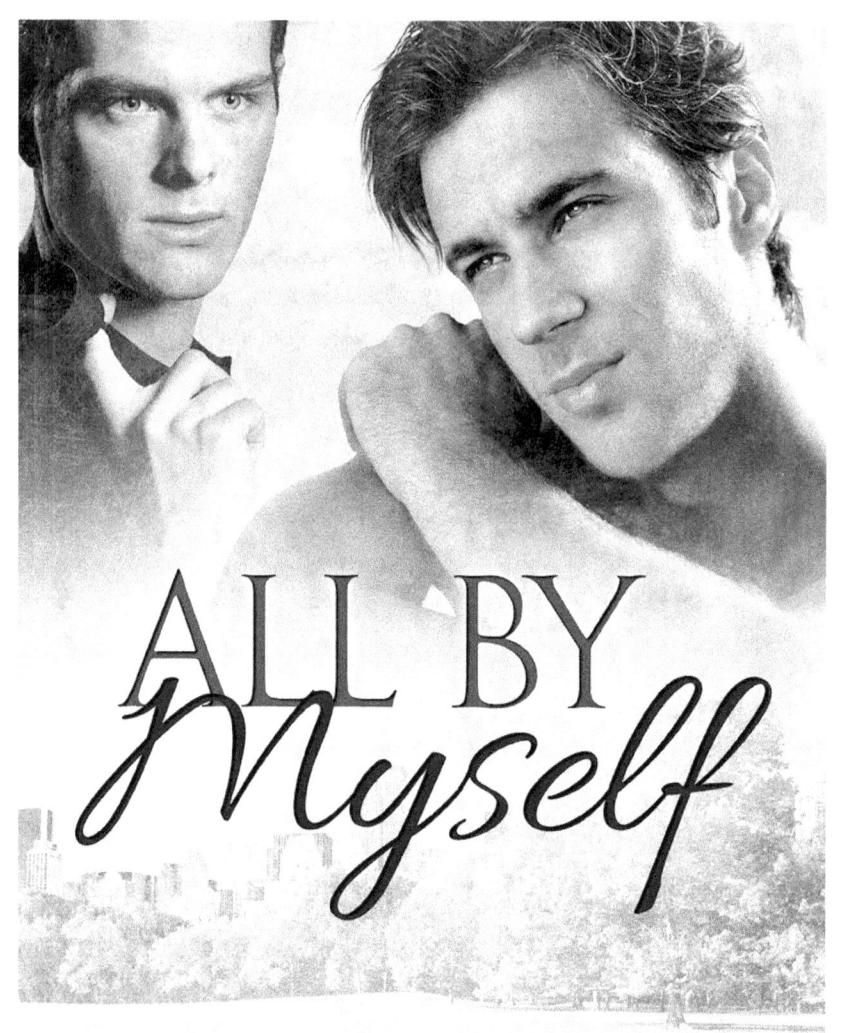

ALL BY Myself

KEN BACHTOLD

http://www.dreamspinnerpress.com

BLINK

Life can change in the blink of an eye.

RICK R. REED

http://www.dreamspinnerpress.com

DIRTY Dining

EM LYNLEY

http://www.dreamspinnerpress.com

http://www.dreamspinnerpress.com

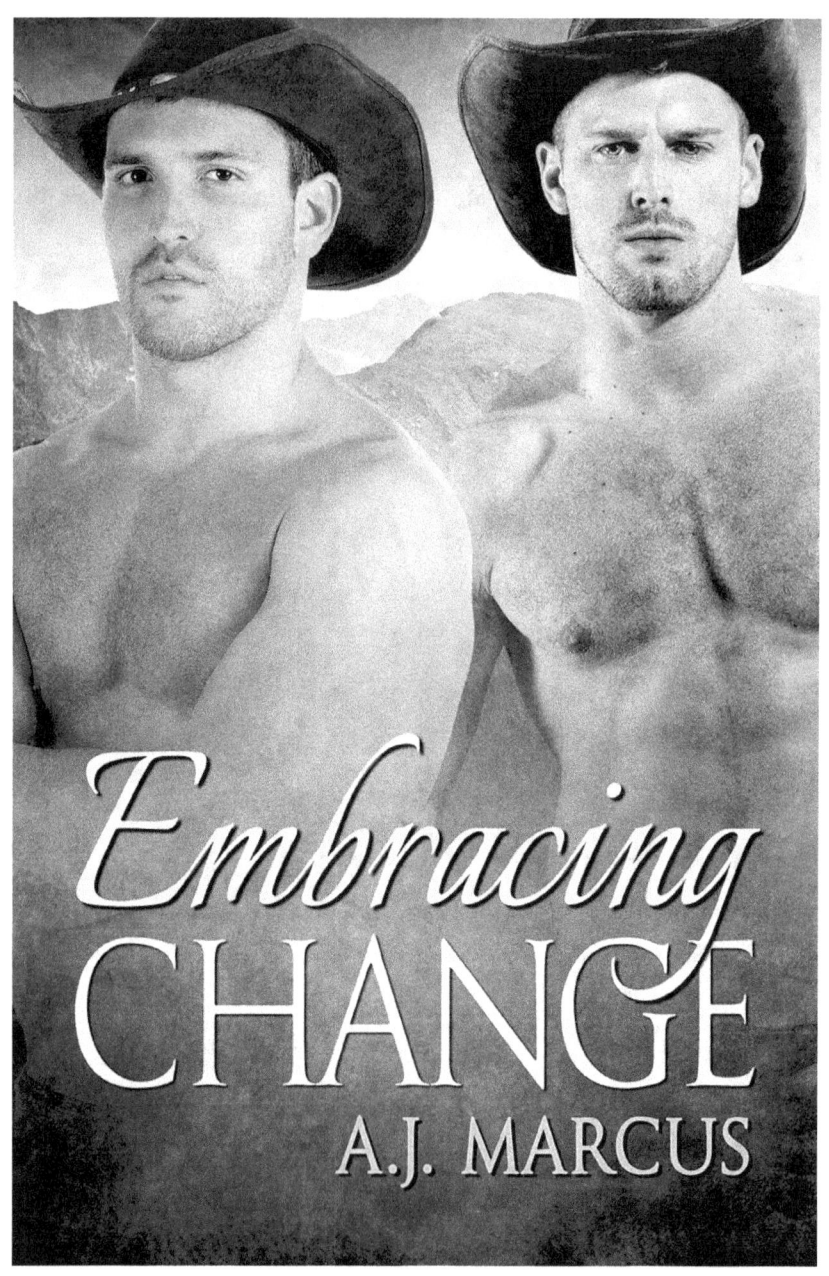

Embracing CHANGE

A.J. MARCUS

http://www.dreamspinnerpress.com

EMERGENCY
CONTACT

ELLE BROWNLEE

http://www.dreamspinnerpress.com

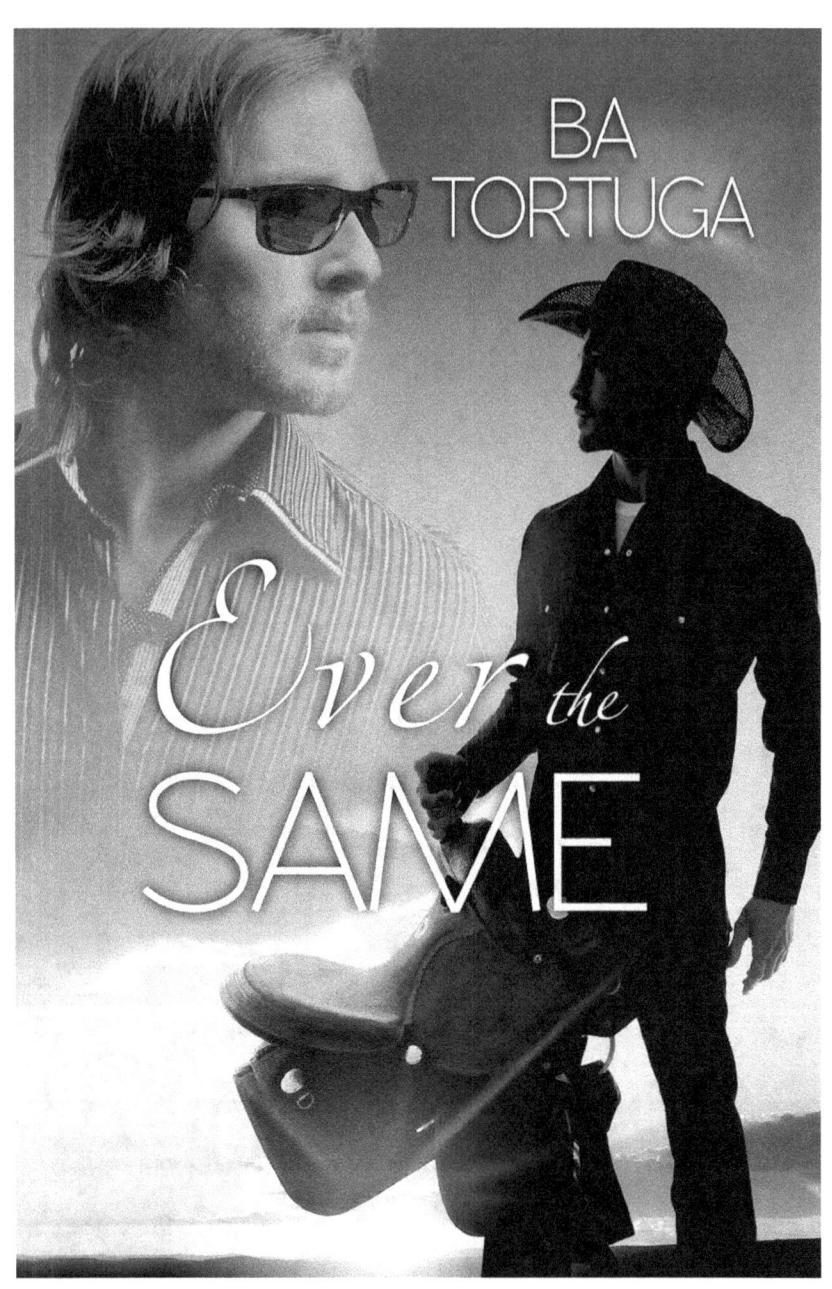

BA
TORTUGA

Ever the
SAME

http://www.dreamspinnerpress.com

FOR **MORE** OF THE **BEST GAY** ROMANCE

Dreamspinner
PRESS
dreamspinnerpress.com

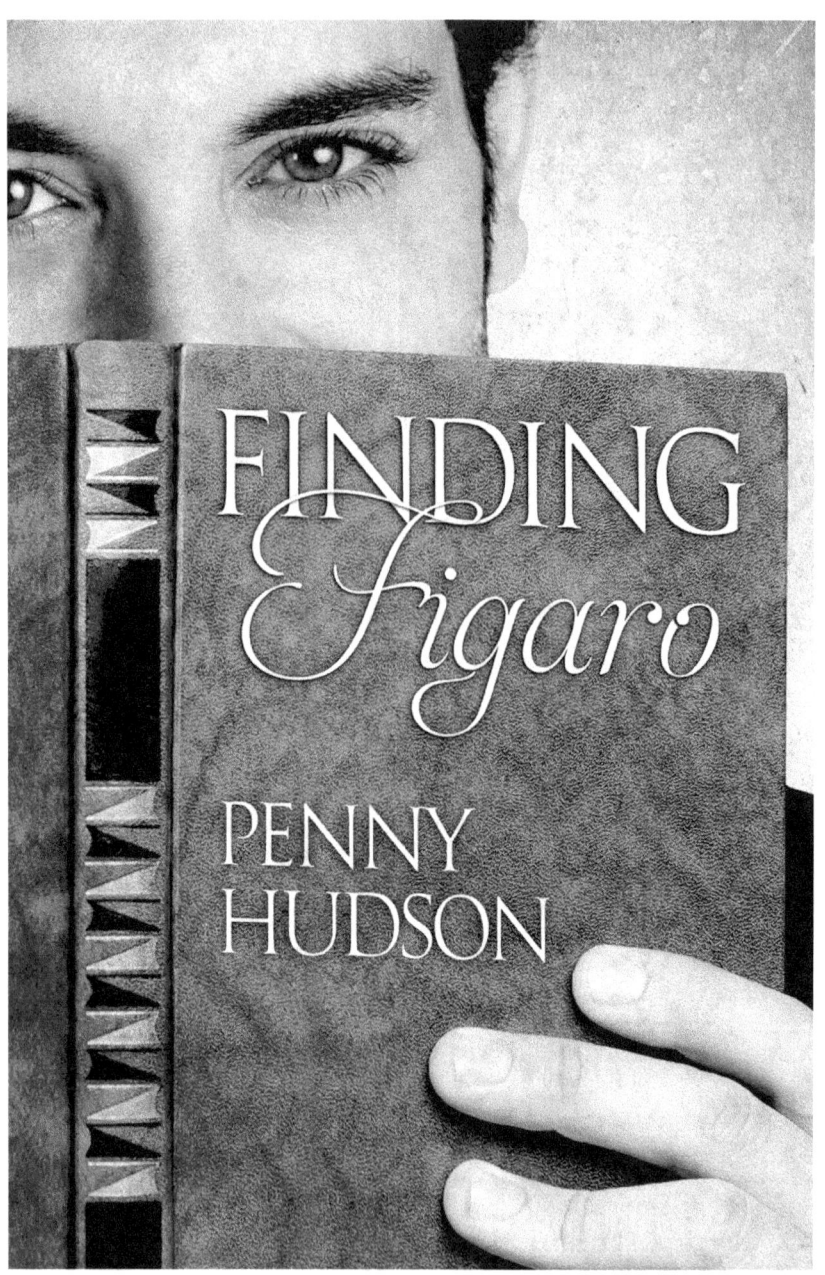

FINDING
Figaro

PENNY
HUDSON

http://www.dreamspinnerpress.com